GIULIANA MORANDINI w.
border with Austria; she now lives in Rome and, occasionally,
Venice. She is particularly interested in the culture of central
Europe and in the relationship between art and the un-
conscious, literature and psychoanalysis.

Morandini became famous in Italy for . . . *E allora mi hanno
rinchiusa* (1977), a poignant investigation of women's mental
hospitals which revealed shocking injustices and was instrumental in changing legislation affecting mental patients.

Other works by Giuliana Morandini include: *La voce che è
in lei* (1980), a study of some 'neglected' 18th- and 19th-
century women writers in Italy; the trilogy consisting of *Cristalli
di Vienna* (1978) winner of the Prato literary prize, *Caffè specchi*
(1983) winner of the Viareggio literary prize, *Angelo a Berlino*
(1987); *Sogno a Herrenberg* (1991) winner of the Flaiano literary
prize; *Giocandoadama con la luna* (1996) finalist for the Bastia
Umbra prize and winner of the Ostia and Latisana literary
prizes. All her novels are published by Bompiani in Italy.

Morandini has also published a collection of poems *Poesie
d'amore* (1986), a reconstruction of the cultural life of Trieste
(*Da te lontano: cultura triestina tra '700 e '800*, 1989), and a
critical edition of *Lettere al padre* (1983), the letters written by
Suor Celeste Galilei to her father. She writes for several Italian
periodicals and is actively engaged in reviews and critical
analysis of literary works from Italy, Germany, central and
eastern Europe.

LUISA QUARTERMAINE is a senior lecturer at the
University of Exeter and has published on Italian literature and
cultures, Renaissance iconography, modern fiction, and film.
She has also worked with the Erasmus Office of the European
Commission in Brussels, coordinating student exchange pro-
grammes. She is at present completing a study of the *Repubblica
di Salo*, the last two years of the Italian fascist government.

THE CAFE OF MIRRORS

Giuliana Morandini

Translated from the Italian
by
Luisa Quartermaine

UNIVERSITY
of
EXETER
PRESS

First published in 1997 by
University of Exeter Press
Reed Hall, Streatham Drive
Exeter, Devon EX4 4QR
UK

© Originally published as *Caffè Specchi*,
© Gruppo Editoriale Fabbri-Bompiani,
Milan, 1983. This English translation
and the Introduction © Luisa Quartermaine 1997.

The cover illustration shows Adrienne (Woman with Bangs),
by Amedeo Modigliani, Chester Dale Collection,
© Board of Trustees, National Gallery of Art,
Washington, 1917, oil on linen.

British Library Cataloguing in Publication Data
A catalogue record for this book is
available from the British Library

ISBN 0 85989 469 X

Typeset in 10/12pt Adobe Caslon by
Kestrel Data, Exeter

Printed and bound in Great Britain by
Short Run Press Ltd, Exeter

Acknowledgements

This translation would not have been possible without the support of the Italian Cultural Institute in London and the help of friends and colleagues, above all of Laura Lepschy. Details on the career of Clara Katharina Pollaczek were kindly provided by Professor W. E. Yates. My husband, Peter, looked at the whole of the translation in its various stages several times (last, appropriately enough, on a research visit of his own to Trieste). I am particularly grateful to Simon Baker, Publisher at the University of Exeter Press, for reading the entire text, commenting very perceptively on it and indicating a number of improvements.

Above all, though, I am grateful to Giuliana Morandini herself: for her time, enthusiasm and generosity of spirit; for coffee, dinner and conversation in Rome, Leuven, Brussels, Venice and London; for answering all my many queries and for the rewarding challenges her book sets any reader or translator.

Notwithstanding help received, any shortcomings in the present translation are mine alone.

L.Q.
Exeter
September 1995

Introduction
by Luisa Quartermaine

Estrangement from the world, that lonely life of the individual which threatens modern existence, informs Giuliana Morandini's fiction. A writer with diverse talents—critic, essayist and novelist—and holder of several literary prizes for her novels, Morandini has found inspiration for her work above all in the culture of *Mitteleuropa*, while Triestine literature and psychoanalysis have given her novels views and perspectives at once diverse and specific.

Her stories have little plot, minimal characterization, and scant action or moral aspect. Their decisive feature is a fundamental shift of perspective from an interest in the world of objects to an examination of the regarding mind; density and opacity is characteristic of her novels, reflection its result.

In her search for expression Morandini often combines shattered images of a desolate environment with the vacuous chattering of incomprehensible languages. Her descriptions are composite constructions, drawn from diverse recollections which no longer give a clear indication of their origins. Within this framework develops the atmosphere of suspended pessimism characteristic of Morandini's work.

The Café of Mirrors (*Caffè specchi*) is typical; devoid of substantial action, with only a subtle thread of events connected with the arrival in town of Katharina, waiting to meet her lawyer over the custody of her son. Hers is a lethargic, passive submission set against an enigmatic city dominated by water—the sea and the rain—and wind. Reflections in the mirrors of its recognizable *caffè* identify it as Trieste; fleeting, yet precise references to its history confirm this identification as correct.

A unique feature of this city is its geographical location. The closest seaport for a large section of central Europe, easily accessed because of the low passes in the mountains to the north at the eastern end of the Alps, Trieste became a point of contact as well as collision of three great cultural and ethnic streams: Latin, Slavonic and Germanic.

But the city landscape is shaped also by the inner thoughts and memories of the protagonist, Katharina Pollaczek. Her name mirrors the geography of the place, a fractured city with an uneasy mosaic of races and languages. Less obviously, Katharina is also the fictional descendant of Clara Katharina Pollaczek (née Loeb) who lived a troubled life in Vienna at the turn of the century and knew the main literary figures of that city. A writer herself, she worked with Hugo von Hofmannsthal (1874–1929) and was closely associated with the writer Arthur Schnitzler (1862–1931) with whom she had an often unhappy relationship.

In its tangle of historical problems, the Trieste of the novel reflects the fragmented personality of the protagonist, images her own crisis.

The two forces, though, that in the novel effectively destroy the concreteness of forms, and deny sense of a fixed point of view, are light (with its calculated study of colour) and reflections (the title of the book acts as a constant reminder). The interaction of light and the multiple reflections of images create an environment of relentless uncertainty. Everything is scrutinized, from the drops of milk on the marble surface of a table or blood seeping through the cracks of a pavement, to coins or butterflies obsessively collected. Morandini's writing blurs the boundaries between the figurative and abstract in a calculated and ambiguous way; at once classical and surreal, her city is refined through amassed details offered with lingering tenderness and melded in the grey evening light of winter.

Trieste's position has made it an inevitable site of contention between Italy, the German-speaking Habsburg Empire and the Slavs. The 'Slav peril' in particular had been an acknowledged fear since the early nineteenth century, together with the threat that Trieste might one day be claimed as an outpost of a Slovene state. This tension was explored by Giuliana Morandini in her 1989 study on Trieste, *Da te lontano*, as the 'crisi interiore della città' [the internal crisis of the city]. She saw it as primarily the consequence of the transition from an ethos based on trade to that created by industry, with its inevitable social implications, but it was also shaped by the antagonistic views of the nationalist movement and the demand that the city should retain links with the Danube hinterland.

This sense of history, together with the feeling of old and stable value systems disintegrating, is reflected in Katharina's own sense of impending crisis: "Again something had to happen, and the uncertainty, the drawing out of time frightened her" (p. 7).

The vision of the city is rigorously mapped. Like the palimpsest of whitewashed walls of Katharina's hotel room, the city reflects a multi-layered society and appears distorted by the fear of the unknown. "Yes, coat upon coat saves on colour they say. And the paint becomes thicker. The layers are like history. You write over it, on everything, black lines cover the facts" (p. 5). Ultimately Katharina herself seems in a state of suspension, aimlessly wandering the streets of Trieste. Her own conviction is that nothing is quite as it seems: "We touch things," she told herself, "to discover closed scenes, the hidden depths beneath the surface. By feeling our way over a huge belly again we rediscover its unfulfilled yearnings" (p. 10).

The volatile atmosphere of a once-great, but now decayed, trading centre accentuates insecurity. This is a location of geographical frontiers, a space of individual life but also of literal as well as metaphorical borders.

Frontier life entails separation, dislocation of family structures, alienation. Existence itself assumes the status of an 'outsider'. The opposition evoked between the crumbling urban architecture and the empty spaces of the city's outskirts draws upon the imagery of a 'doleful city', not a city for the living, but a necropolis, a mental hell.

"During these last few days, walking around the city, [. . .] I have thought about the exterminations carried out . . . just on the outskirt of this city . . . the sea still seems to be veiled with ash . . . and nobody wants to talk about it . . ."
"This city is sinking into the shadows . . . with its factories and silent sirens . . . there are no descendants . . ." (p. 124).

Apathy and indolence, hidden elements which threaten existence, are juxtaposed with new encounters and flash-backs which, rather than an accessory to the story, are its central focus. "To perceive," said Bergson, "is after all nothing more than the opportunity to remember."

Morandini's narrative style images the mind's language, exploiting its capacity for association and sequent observation as well as its ability to manipulate images while constantly admitting new material.

What Katharina (and through her Morandini) strives for is an empathy with the world of things, an identity between objects and emotions. Her focus is on experience rather than external objects, her sensibility accords emotional value to a mechanized world in a constant interplay between subject and environment where dream and reality are one, reaching a symbiosis where neither dominates. To this complex relationship Morandini brings her individual perception of place and space, a perception which changes the object perceived.

> "I would like to touch physically what happens to me . . .
> but the noise would remain . . . I'm afraid of its thickness
> . . . of being encircled . . . It was like this in the garden
> that enclosed me as a child . . . it had a high wall, damp
> and dark bricks, I did not go out . . . and the voices rose
> without my being able to see anything . . ." (p. 53).

The nature of this experience, the discrepancy between truth and appearances, is sharpened in the novel by the language used; never too realistic, its style develops through assonance, association, sounds, and colours. Morandini renders visible what cannot be reasoned logically; concrete objects lose the materiality of still life: "our images are always so out of focus and retain only the threads of our desires" (p. 51). Semantic ambiguity distorts reality; truth is unobtainable.

Deserted and ominous spaces within the city shade into mental anguish, abstract ideas. Physical distance evokes distant times and lands. No-one lives behind the arcades; glass doors reflect dark, empty roads; the *bora* sweeps away any vestige of life; pavements are broken; building sites, where abandoned plaster has solidified, stand inactive as frozen moments of catastrophy; everything is static, even the sea or the dancing figure Katharina recollects in her hotel bedroom. Figuratively this is the land beyond time, a primordial landscape of wilderness and desert.

Morandini's portrait of misery and death (as in the description in the novel of the dead Serbian girl) shows a visual awareness of European pictorial tradition. Bringing together German Expressionism with the timeless architecture of early twentieth-century *Newe Sachlishkeit*, Morandini endows urban life with a sense of rigidity and alienation. Her city is a collaged space with unsettling perspectives and displaced horizons, a paradoxical world of contradictions between secure, recognizable references and an alien townscape peopled by faceless encounters. As in De Chirico's paintings, objects stripped of their usual function, context and meaning assume new ones. Even the most familiar seems estranged, remote and immobile. The squares and the streets are those of Trieste once removed; like the silent images of De Chirico's Italian *piazze* and streets they reveal the same nostalgia and yearning for the northern world—Munich in the case of De Chirico, Vienna in the case of Morandini.

Aside from the fascination of its artistic life, what Vienna offered Morandini through its history and rituals was the living synthesis of irreconcilable opposites: a contemporary world inextricably linked to the past. Hidden under the surface, scarcely mentioned, yet clearly perceptible is the typical preoccupation of fin-de-siècle Vienna, the erotic seen as a physical attraction, but also—at once disturbing and exciting—the perception of its distinctive climate of change. A world of obsession lies behind the seductive façade of the old city: "All is well at the court in Vienna" is the ironic reminder in the novel, where the nostalgia for "old" Vienna is combined with a sarcastic criticism of its conservatism and empty rituals:

> The horses run wild carrying the uncovered body of the little Polish countess, Maria. The prince's death is in order. The court is in mourning, the emperor orders preparations to be made for going to Bad Ischl. Another waltz (p. 5).

In Trieste, once part of the Austrian Empire, nothing could be further away from this pre-ordained pattern of existence; there is no established path for Katharina to follow. Morandini evokes a past no longer attainable while the fear of modern life is emphasized in the rigid, airless spaces where human endeavour shrinks to an impenetrable world of objects. People, too, are awkward players in a charade whose meaning is lost. Still rooted in the past, Katharina's life has become restless and unstable. This insecurity helps to explain the melancholy expressed for her childhood, but also her distance from the present—a vision of which is neither perfectly defined nor completely expressed.

The sense of approaching disaster, the inconsequentiality of a society held together only by conventions and an antiquated code of honour, has its counterpart in the dissolution of the language. This theme had already been explored at length by Arthur Schnitzler and Hugo von Hofmannsthal. Echoing the works of these writers, Katharina's own unspoken thoughts make apprehensible that collapse of moral sense which results from the alienation of the individual within society.

Cities should celebrate communication and living together: "Men came to cities to live," said Aristotle, "and stayed to live a better life." When language breaks down, the city itself begins to crumble. Through the dissolution of syntax and of logical discourse Morandini reflects the degeneration of society, her use of language disconcerts and unsettles the reader.

There is deliberate eclecticism, and an almost manneristic opulence in her writing. If her syntax seems to negate the literary convention of classical novels, her style is full of ambiguities and personal mythologies, and draws strongly from examples of early twentieth-century art in a continuum of responses to cultural traditions. Plain at times, mordant and even baroque more often—and with a wry tinge of nostalgia—her writing is a blend of impasto techniques, not easily accessible. As in her other novels, *The Café of Mirrors* establishes several perspectives which go beyond its immediate setting and subject matter. It deals with the disintegration of the past, the uncertainty of the present and the courage needed to embrace a future.

Historical Note on the City of Trieste
Of Roman origins and initially under Venice, the city passed into Austrian hands at the end of the fourteenth century but, unlike many other Austrian territories, it retained a great deal of autonomy. Politically, however, the city began to evolve only in the eighteenth century when, during the reign of Maria Theresa (the Maria Theresia mentioned in the novel) and Francis II, the *Erbländer* (autonomous districts within the Austrian

Empire) began to increase in power and importance. Once Venice and the crumbling Ottoman Empire had been dealt with, Austria had finally an open route into the Adriatic. It was the mercantilistic policies practised by a succession of Austrian monarchs which determined Trieste's importance as a port city. Its significance as an expanding foreign trade centre was highlighted in 1719 when Trieste was given the status of *Porto Franco* (free port). At its peak it was the third most important port in the Mediterranean after Marseille and Genoa.

The racial composition of the city remained mixed. The Slovenes, who had originally dominated the hills round Trieste and the surrounding countryside, continued to do so. In the town, however, Italian was spoken and this was also the language of the administration and of sea trade. Moreover, the Austrians allowed the Italians within Trieste to assert their influence both politically and economically over the Slavs and the port itself to acquire an essentially Italian character. Thus the city became a point of intense rivalry among the German-speaking Austrians to the north (who desired the city as a seaport to the upper Danubian area), the Slavic-speaking people of the north east (who claimed the right to control over the region inhabited mainly by Slovenians), and the Italians who asserted hegemony by virtue of the Italian population living in Trieste and of the predominantly Italian urban structure of the city.

Despite the rapid expansion of the port, Trieste's importance was short-lived. Its fragility, together with the growing weakness of the Habsburg Empire, was initially exposed when it was occupied twice by Napoleon's troops (and annexed to the French Empire for a short while), and more recently when its significance as a trading centre within the Austrian Empire was gradually replaced by better-equipped northern German ports, such as Hamburg.

The collapse of the Austrian Empire after World War I left the doors of Trieste open to the Italians, but its fate and its impending isolation were not altered. With World War II, Trieste became a bone of contention between Italy, Germany and Yugoslavia, and the city declined further.

Since 1954, when Trieste was made part of Italy and the regional capital of the Friuli-Venezia Giulia area, its population has continued to fall, with Italians emigrating abroad and being replaced by refugees from Istria under former Yugoslavian rule.

The recent collapse of the communist regimes of the eastern bloc countries, and the civil and ethnic wars in neighbouring territories of the ex-Yugoslavia, have once again propelled the city into the news. Indeed the war between Slovenes and Serbs brought the fighting very near to the frontier, filling the city's hospital with casualties. Trieste is now in the process of forging new trade and political links with both Croatia and Slovenia. At the same time there is talk of Trieste becoming an offshore centre trading once again with the eastern countries. History might repeat itself, after all.

Translator's Note

In order to maintain the character of the city described in this novel, and to respect the author's stylistic choice, the dialogues in dialect and the phrases in a language other than Italian have been left untranslated in the text with a translation provided in footnotes. Where English was used in the original this has been identified by the use of italic.

Spiegel: noch nie hat man wissend beschrieben,
was ihr in euerem Wesen seid.
Ihr, wie mit lauter Löchern von Sieben
erfüllten Zwischenräume der Zeit . . .

RAINER MARIA RILKE,
Aus den Sonetten an Orpheus, II, 3

1

Against the pallor of the city where large buildings fronted the sea she made out a solitary, green dome. She recognized the columns eaten away by salty air, the statues like cardboard cutouts against the sky.

Only when the dark car stopped before the hotel did she hesitate. She would have gone on, but the taxi driver had already unloaded her suitcase.

The man she met was wearing a uniform too big for him. He seemed suspended from a hook, or perhaps he had only lost weight. He stood slightly stooped, and when he fumbled for his round glasses in the back pocket of his trousers, he pushed aside the flap of his uniform.

She stood still, the big bag slung over her shoulder, feeling the buckle cutting into her skin. The flesh there was already bruised. To change position had become impossible. She was in that state of mind when, after a sharp blow, immobility is the only reaction possible. She felt as if someone was pushing her forward, or maybe it was the draught from the revolving glass door, which rotated like the cylinder of some optical instrument. Her bag slipped off, pulling her towards Reception.

The unknown faces of people passing before her were reassuring. The gangly shape of an Englishman went in front of her:

"*Good morning*," he said in English. "*I wonder if you have a single room with bath.*"

Not wishing to interrupt the remoteness that the English language gave, she also spoke in English:

"My name is Katharina Pollaczek. Last night Mr Osermann reserved a room for me. Would you mind checking under my name?"

"I have just noticed your name because it's a very strange one," answered the young man in an accent learnt at school. He had a thin moustache, and reddish down on his chin.

"Well, it's just like any other name."

The young man pressed a bell but nobody came.

Katharina said: *"No, don't worry. I can find my own way."*

The lift welcomed her with its flowery ironwork. A slow ascent past empty floors and soft corridors carpeted purple.

On her floor someone stealthily entered a room. She saw the position of the knees, so bent one doubted they could ever straighten again. Either the person was greeting someone important or the bones had bowed that way in childhood.

She looked at the faded blind. She watched it fill gently in the cold wind coming off the sea. An unusual pole, like those used in a gymnasium, supported it. She felt the urge to do physical exercises. Had they not, after all, taught her to dance at the age of four? "It is good for the body," they said, "even if you don't become a ballerina."

The steps became movements studied according to music, and gestures followed the prints of the upturned feet. The minuets were torture; how could one envisage a happy childhood?

"With this pole one could invent a new movement," she smiled. "It has its good sides being up there, balancing on the bar, on your pointes, touching the ceiling with your head. One feels warmer, something sweet envelopes you, it's the compressed air." She loved to have a bird's-eye view of rooms. She always did it, when she was sitting and waiting.

The room had only been cleaned, it had not seen decorators but had been hurriedly whitewashed. Yes, coat upon coat saves on colour, they say. And the paint becomes thicker. The layers are like history. You write over it, on everything, black lines cover the facts . . . *und Gott stehe uns bei.*[1] Stucco crumbles and plaster comes loose, it is all part of the inevitable. What matters is to save appearances, one gives a quick clean. What one shows is not what is, just as in the best murders the face of those giving the orders remains unknown, so that nothing changes. "All is well at the court in Vienna. The horses run wild carrying the uncovered body of the little Polish countess, Maria. The prince's death is in order. The court is in mourning, the emperor orders preparations to be made for going to Bad Ischl. Another waltz; the women dance on tiptoe, repeating their magic circles in space; their movements, dictated by etiquette, are clouds of powder in the night air."

She did not open her case. Left everything untouched. Washed her hands with rough soap. Her skin flaked.

---

[1] And God be with us.

She went downstairs on foot, past empty floors. She sat by the expanse of glass to look at the sea.

A woman dressed in vivid, contrasting colours, from red to purple, was waiting to cross the avenue. She turned her face carelessly towards the glass entrance; her face was still pretty, with high cheek bones and grey eyes. Katharina felt herself observed. The woman picked up the bag she had put on the ground, the wind stirred her coloured skirt and her figure swayed a little, unsteady, perhaps not only because of the wind. She kept on walking slowly and went away.

The noise of the sea came as far as the large window. The ceiling flooded with the glow, but the rest of the room was sunk in shadow. The dark street lamps broke the line of the water and the air was agitated by the flight of seagulls.

"The wind always comes back . . . but why does fear begin again?" "Yes," she searched a long way back. "When I came to this city . . ." She rediscovered the girl who ran away from those abandoned things, from those figures who no longer had a face. She had left for the Orient, where boundaries disappeared and the wind wore away their traces.

A distant dream recurred, a huge sky, vaster than in any other place, a dome enlarged by bright frescoes. She was staring at the horizon, motionless in its reflection, full of apprehension, she who loved the blue sky and the mountains brought close by limpid air. But that morning in July the clouds were white, murmuring among themselves and one, higher than the rest, was proudly teasing the smaller strays. She was looking at the road, the grey colour of the granite was more friendly than that un- compromising light. Those few items of make-up in the wicker basket she had as a young bride would dispel her pallor but not the dark circles round her eyes. Her life was changing and with the determination of a simple girl she sought a few crumbs of happiness. But above her the blue was deep.

"A familiar fear . . . And when the wind drops, one must wait." Again something had to happen, and the uncertainty, the drawing out of time frightened her. "And yet I am here for a precise reason," she convinced herself. "I have an appointment with the lawyer for the custody of my son Friedrich."

She wanted to walk without being seen, she tried to do this but it was a great effort when other people's eyes met hers. She endured the contact with people and this tired her, the lump in her throat grew bigger. It was because of a certain intensity on the part of the hotel staff, in the way they looked at her.

She avoided those eyes which stopped her thinking and looking at the sea, the only thing she longed for. She ordered tea and cakes.

The waiter approached quietly, watching her. Katharina searched for something to say but nothing came to her lips, she could not articulate with the vague movements of her swelling tongue. The man looked at her openly, demanding attention, but she kept staring at the glass door, even when he carelessly banged down the last piece of the tea-set, scraping it against the green marble top of the table.

"One more scratch," thought Katharina.

Some milk dripped from the spout, stood like a chalk button.

The waiter went away, his footsteps leaving no trace on the thick carpet.

She took a cake. "I haven't eaten any for a long time," she thought. They were flat and icy cold like pottery. "They must be false . . . How odd to think of winter and cakes."

Those cakes she used to eat as a child. Her house did not look onto the sea, but down into the square. Her nanny Cerovka would enter a few minutes before her mother, the expression on her face clearly heralding some decision which affected her. Behind Cerovka came her mother; one could hear her voice before she was in the room, a voice to which one was not able to respond except with silence. It planned the day as always: "Today you will not go out with Cerovka." "Not even to school?" she would ask; for even though she knew the answer she liked to make sure. "No, not even to school . . . the *bora*[1] is as strong as ever." She would remain only for a second so that her voice hung in the air, suspended.

Katharina used to look forward to the scene behind the cold glass. She would suck her fingers, sticky with *kolaci* and run barefoot to the window. She would press her face against the glass to have a better view upwards.

In the swollen sky, taut to the limit, dark furrows like veins of tin and lead laced the purple vault, sketched the outline of the storm in every direction. The clouds divided across a map ruled by magnetic fields.

---

[1] Very strong, cold wind which blows along the north-east coast of Italy. (Tr.)

In the room the delicate smoke not drawn in by the fireplaces exuded the resins of Slovenian woods. The stove whistled as if, instead of wood, they had fed it wolves.

"Listen," Cerovka invited her to lend an ear, "the voice comes down from the mountain."

"Whose voice is it?"

"The brothers from Carso have come down to the sea to fight and die and their sister cries for them."

"Does she wait for them on the rocks?"

"No," recounted Cerovka patiently, "she has swollen, has become big, has flown along the gorges . . . it is the *bora*."

The *bora* was approaching, oppressing the landscape with its power. One could not see her; she could be recognized by the houses, the roofs where she took command; her fury grew as she swept through the attics; the lofts let themselves be taken, seduced by her impetuous and extravagant folly; the streets behind her were unrecognizable. She would take the form of a witch mad with excitement while she cleaned and recleaned the market square. The pavement shone like a bald head and the mad gusts left behind a white emptiness. The sky was becoming cold and dull in colour and the roofs under the arches looked black and curved, full of expectation. For Katharina, the lone spectator, little figures appeared on the wild stage, marionettes pulled by a thread that had escaped from the puppeteer's hands, clinging to the stone walls, their cloaks assuming every bizarre shape enjoyed by the wind.

Her breath was steaming and the window panes, no longer frozen, misted with little clouds of water.

She brushed insistently against the marble, she had always liked the coldness of its veins, a break from thinking. Besides, its friable edges sharpened a childish curiosity.

"We touch things," she told herself, "to discover closed scenes, the hidden depths beneath the surface. By feeling our way over a huge belly again we rediscover its unfulfilled yearnings."

She knew how to measure the emptiness which yawned behind things and the membrane of thoughts. If nature rejected some rules, there remained the possibility of experimenting. The images were insistent even when a veil covered them. And the geometrical constructions seemed themselves to be linked to ancient figures, to a measure of things that attractions and disappointments established in childhood; through separation those designs made survival possible.

She opened and closed her leather bag. The objects it held seemed to her different each time, like the repetition of experiments in a laboratory. If one could not achieve exactness, it would be perseverance in verifications that would reassure. She would try to cope with the future which the woman could detect from the cards she had in her bag; the brightly coloured woman could go away.

She looked around again; she, too, was sitting still like them. "Perhaps we are chrysalises," and she checked, lightly brushing her cheek. "We need words; they offer us a structure, it does not matter if often they slip past the meaning."

Outside, the wind resumed its mischievous game. It enjoyed blowing against the glass partition on the right and, at regular intervals, swept the dust away. The line that enclosed the sea disappeared and the effort of gazing at it became fruitless.

The archaeologist, who had arrived when Maria Theresia's engineers were planning the harbour, had to wait for a long time. His pale eyes were scrutinizing the depths, imagining the underwater objects. Ships were at anchor in the harbour. His dream was wearing thin, no beauty came any more to meet his desire. He walked along the narrow alleys behind the harbour and found old words among the new ones exchanged in the Greek coffee bars. One of the golden coins he had was so shiny that it reflected images like a mirror. Turning it in his hand, he caught the eye of the young man who was following him.

"Loneliness brings only punishment," she said to herself, and turned her face abruptly towards the inside. The room was immense, the view lost in the distance.

Someone was reading the newspaper in the special *Zeitungsspanner*[1] which, when held upright, could hide people's faces. Behind the still pages one could see only the legs of the dozing bodies, and occasionally a hand which, raised in the shadow, looked like marble.

"I shall drink my tea now," she said to herself, "otherwise it will go cold." And she felt a shiver. "My hand is warm and touches the marble. I am able to look far away."

"The wind carries the cries of the seagulls." Her thoughts were wandering. "I must have cried like that once . . . when I had the baby." She could see again the grey doors that could be opened only from within. Men with masked faces were pushing the trolley, whispering. Her belly threw those voices back. They asked her about

---

[1] The term refers to the piece of wood which, particularly in coffeebars and libraries of the Austrian area, is fixed to newspapers in order to make reading easier.

II

her husband. She made an effort to forget the burning pain. She saw the blue sky again, a white wicker basket. She tried to lift her hand but her arms were linked to a thin tube in which ran a red liquid. The door was banging in the wind. They kept talking and her name lingered. They were saying that they needed authorization. "Nevertheless we must operate," they concluded. They held her by the shoulders, the red tube was running fast. Her belly was burning and a scorching disc was getting closer, attacking her. Bandaged men covered in beams of moonlight were around that sun . . .

It was becoming dark. The waiter had left the bill on the tray. She did not pay.

A street lamp came on. The sudden light hurt.

The drop of spilt milk on the table had divided. Two snow-white drops looked at her like pupils from the green table-top, and the hand of the man in a surgeon's coat rose pointing a finger, her name was called out, the eyes were not moonbeams but blades.

The wind outside was easing a little.

She would have liked her body to follow her longings and feelings of nostalgia. Like this, motionless, she found it difficult to ease her anxiety.

Darkness was settling on the readers, blurring their outlines. Those silent bodies respected her presence.

The faces watching her had a sallow colour. She thought of chlorine, she loved the colours of the substances mixed in the test tube. "They remain the same," each time she was amazed, "and change only at the moment of the reaction." In contact with the hydrogen, the chlorine comes alive. Two worlds embrace, but the life of the acid suffers.

The men who kept to the rules had foreseen a sense of vertigo. The weight that escapes dependence loses its identity. A physicist from Vienna dressed as a poet knew this. He used to walk by the harbour, as the gypsies still tell, and loved his world of paper and figures. "Truth," he would say, "must be attained through secret paths." People would laugh at him as if his accounts of physics were hallucinated lines of poetry in a moonlit night. The brightly coloured woman turns her cards to tell the future, and speaks of the gangling figure who always wore the same discoloured clothes. The cards touch the marble of the table. Now Katharina wants to know and the Slav gypsy turns the card over; the figure is upside down. "Yes," answers the gypsy, "it was a day when the wind pushed its season forward. It was the same day when the sea cast ashore a pair of dead dolphins." "Ah, the physicist from Vienna," people whispered. "Se sa, il vento no se bon con chi non lo conossi!"[1]

"The mirrors are everywhere . . . ," thought Katharina, ". . . it's impossible to escape attention . . . it was useless to feign blindness . . . when silence stretched over the Carso, the Slovenian peasant rebelled against the fate of the Empire and white stones rolled to support his voice, their rustic sound sought to break that stubborn darkness."

"Useless to ask whether any messages have arrived." She looked at the young man with the thin reddish moustache and crew-cut; was he a replacement for the old porter? "Leopold," she remembered, "had a uniform with braid. He was proud of wearing his peaked hat and, at night,

---

[1] "It's obvious, the wind is not kind to those who don't know it!"

13

the lamp light on his chest." Now the young porter's complex irritations resulted in his not recording any messages.

She wanted to know about Leopold, about his health. "When is he coming back to work? And what if finally he has to give up his job?" "In that case," she thought, "the hotel itself will not last long."

The young man shook his round, pumpkin head in small jerks. The straight moustache hid his lips, thin slits in a wall. It was becoming difficult to ask him anything. That mouth could not answer. Moreover, Katharina had forgotten the questions. She thought of Leopold. "He would understand when someone was waiting for messages. If they did not come he seemed to make them up. To put someone at rest he might give almost any message."

She endured the proximity of that presence, feeling annoyed at the sense of immobility. The large shoulders were totally visible, he was different from the shapes of the readers.

To observe matter that was uniform and non-malleable frightened her. Meanwhile the wait was tearing her apart.

2

Dusk had fallen. Silent waiters lit lamps on the tables, illuminating only limited areas of no interest.

A man stopped reading, put down the newspaper, its pages stretched like silk. He was tall, with long, unsteady legs. He made as if to go for a stroll rather than to walk far, crossing his hands behind his back.

Outside, an ambulance passed at speed.

Katharina was waiting for her solicitor, Mr Osermann, to ring. He was to come the next day. Leopold, too, would be back.

She went out. She followed the reflection of the railway track that ran parallel to the stone edge, behind which the water was silent. She lengthened her stride. She wanted to move away from the seafront and leave those faces in the darkness. She turned inland following the canal where the hulls of the boats were creaking and bumping one against the other.

In the alley where the ashlar blocks ended, she met the waiter Klaus. He was coming out of a low, tiny door. Dressed as he was, without his uniform, she thought he was someone else. Seeing her outside the hotel, he must have thought the same, because he seemed not to recognize her and did not greet her. He only lowered his head, an allusion to something. Or maybe he could not be bothered to do more. He had a polished leather bag under his arm, which he carefully put down on the ground in order to close the door.

Where the canal ended, she moved on through streets which were all alike, between light-coloured houses which the wind had made porous as sponges. Several large buildings were decorated with timeless statues and pediments. The face of the city was like an exhibition of photographs, and she wondered what lay behind each exposure, what lurked behind the façades and the network of streets.

To walk like this was to offer oneself up to injury.

She passed in front of a coffee bar. There was noise. They were discussing some event of the day. She wanted to stop, but immediately felt that she was confronted by something serious that would prevent her waiting.

She took another alley which rose towards Donota Street. She kept walking slowly even when music came out of a mezzanine window. It was a nasty, unintelligible piece of music; the screeching of the violin was unbearable, the notes hurt her head. She wanted to complain aloud, as is she were in pain.

The street climbed, narrowing. The windows on the ground floors eyed one another. From the basements came the smell of overcooked food and meals forgotten on stoves by the concierges who were keen to be abreast of the latest events from their doorstep.

Katharina stopped at a corner milkbar. She felt the need of a glass of milk; it was closing time and they refused to serve her. She wanted to keep climbing, but had difficulty in breathing and was thirsty.

The concierges of numbers 15 and 18 were discussing animatedly the incident at the coffee bar at number 9.

The concierge of number 15 seemed understanding:

"Tanto se sa, le xe tute cussì. Se tira tanto la corda fin che quei poveri omini i diventa mati."[1]

The interjection of number 18 sounded drastic:

"Ma no ti vedevi come 'l spetava. La vigniva sempre in ritardo e quel povero fio, a star là a spetar, no'l fazeva che bever."[2]

And number 15:

"Ma cossa vuol dir bever un bicer de più? Xe la rabbia, no? Quel povereto gaveva lassà la famiglia e la mula lo gà cazà via."[3]

The dialogue grew louder and the smell of the neglected cooking pots made her sick. She had stopped a little away from number 15, as if she were looking for an address, when number 18 shouted loudly:

"Torno a dir, se 'ste s'ciave le va su e zò, no se pol viver."[4]

---

[1] We know in any case, they are all the same. They go on and on until, poor men, they lose their heads.

[2] But didn't you see how he kept waiting for her? She was always late and that poor bloke, there, always waiting for her, and drinking while he waited.

[3] But what does it mean to drink one glass more? It's the anger, isn't it? That poor fellow had left his family and the girl threw him out.

[4] I repeat, if these Slavs keep going backwards and forwards, it can't go on.

The women's words were getting confused, like pebbles in gravel. Katharina felt sick, she walked on past those two numbers.

She looked fruitlessly in her handbag in search of something. With her head leaning against the bag, she could smell the acid leather. Her hand groped among the invisible and forgotten objects relishing the contact of each of them, one by one. They belonged to her and helped her surmount that wall between herself and the concierge of number 18.

She raised her eyes towards the first floor windows; a young boy had his nose pressed against the glass. She could not see his features but imagined a little, wide face flattened by the cold, transparent surface. The other windows were closed and the cracks in the plaster attacked their edges.

She wanted to go back to where she had come from without passing in front of number 9. But people were gathering, the ambulance was having difficulty because of the narrow alley and the crowd of onlookers.

She looked for a support. Went where pushed. She was close, very close to the body. She turned towards a young man:

"Let me come through, I don't want to look."

"It's impossible," he answered without seeing her. "On this side there is the stretcher."

The words were like coarse gravel against the skin of a new-born baby. She listened to someone listing the objects that had fallen from the young girl's handbag, simple little things that were like her, a tiny rabbit squashed by the man in a white coat. Two grey figures arrived carrying a tin bucket, they threw it carelessly on the paving. Meanwhile the blood had seeped into the cracks of the cobblestones.

She looked at the girl's dress. "It's so simple," she thought, "how can one wear a dress like this to die?" It was checked, the open pleats of the skirt allowed a glimpse of a long, firm leg. From the pocket fell cigarettes and a red pencil.

She was young, perhaps twenty. Her right leg was uncovered to the groin, the skin still light pink. A beauty spot on her knee was the only mark imprinted on the long, pale surface.

Katharina looked at the ground as if about to fall; she hoped someone might realize that she was feeling ill. Nobody took any notice.

The buzz of voices revealed a rich cross-section of languages and dialects. Grey figures were dictating useless details to a man dressed in dark clothes. She was struck by the tight, shiny knot in his tie, like a dilated spot on his chest.

She looked elsewhere, away from those cardboard cut-out figures. Her eyes met with the boy's; he was still nearby. Without understanding why, she felt certain that he was stopping her from getting through. He was so very close, much taller than herself, with light hair and wide, motionless shoulders, and wore a mottled jumper made of twisted, hairy, rust-coloured wool. The expression in his eyes changed rapidly from kind to cold.

She stared at the man with the shiny tie. The big mark on his throat was getting larger. She remembered the breathing exercises and took a deep breath to rid herself of something. Her nostrils were closing, there were too many people to breathe out; she would not have been able to expel the air that swelled her lungs. The sharp pain came back; she gave up. "A useless operation." The air was therefore free to move and fill her body. She saw her belly inflate like a soap bubble.

The man looked with determination straight into her eyes; maybe his words hung in the air and Katharina could not hear them, or maybe he knew the answer already and was sure of her silence.

The boy with the rust-coloured jumper was with her.

A fat man, panting heavily, the skin down to his throat shining, pushed her forward violently. The heel of her shoe stuck in the drain cover. She was motionless, tensed like an athlete on the point of leaping forward. She had a fit of hysterical laughter; nobody was aware of her discomfort.

Her handbag had fallen to the ground, all of its contents spilled. A great number of things she did not know, but which belonged to her, caught her attention.

A photograph she had not looked at for some time, now yellowed and stained, showed her young son. Was she not there in that city, among unknown people, near a murdered young woman, because of that image? The print had been in contact with something damp and a halo had formed around the face, only the eyes had been left intact and large, Friedrich's eyes.

The young man lifted her almost at arm's length to move her from that position. Her shoe remained stuck.

Katharina gathered her scattered belongings, dirty with mud. Something, the name of which she could not remember, had slipped through the metal grid.

She managed to free the shoe, recovered control of her body. Just in time to let the stretcher go by, moving through the lonely people as if nobody was carrying it.

And then she saw her. She observed her cheekbones,

the oval shape of her face, her mouth with the upper lip round and swollen.

She gave her a last glance and thought of the metal grid that had imprisoned her foot.

The man in the dark suit closed his notebook.

3

The circle of multi-coloured heads around the crime was thinning out. Colourless people wandered about, uncertain while returning to their own occupations. An elderly woman coughed into her handkerchief and placed it back in her handbag, making the metal lock click. Some old women, vegetables poking from their bags, were harping on the details of the incident.

The owner of the coffee bar resumed her position as protagonist behind the high counter. Her fat body wobbled slightly as she was giving out the latest cleaning instructions.

The thin man carrying the bucket filled with foamy water had lived for many years with this woman with the shiny skin. He came in and out several times, his pale face showing a slight trembling, a twitch.

He had long before learnt to obey in silence and now, to the words the woman uttered in quick succession, he answered with a sad face. "Perhaps," Katharina said to herself, "he, too, is thinking that without that presence, the crime might still have happened, but elsewhere."

The stream of blood had been running along parallel and convenient cracks, had spread on the majolica in front of the doorstep. A splatter with raised and irregular edges indicated the pain of the movement brought to a sudden stop.

The man turned to Katharina before tipping the bucket

full of foam, to make sure that no further complaints would be aroused in her look. She smiled, and the man stopped his tic for a second, lowering his head.

The woman behind the counter quickened her tapping of the figures on her machine and without following the man any longer, head bent, exclaimed abruptly:

"No te ga capì mai gnente ne la vita. E adesso te cominci anche a intrigarme sul lavor."[1]

The concierges of numbers 15 and 18 came in.

The one from number 18 had a shrill voice, her arms up to the elbow showed an excessive flabbiness; she was not old and yet, because of her wrinkles and freckles, looked it. Her version of the crime differed greatly from that given by the concierge of number 15, who instead showed sympathy for the victim.

"Torno a dir," insisted the concierge of number 18, "quel che gò sempre dito. Se quelle s'ciave le stessi a casa sua, noi stessimo meio."[2]

As she went out, Katharina felt as if that flabby arm had touched her.

Behind the door nobody had yet lifted the overturned chair from which the girl had fallen. Stuck to the base was her red scarf. Katharina picked it up, nobody saw her, and she wrapped it round her throat. She felt the dampness and waited for the man to finish with the foamy water so that he could bring her some wine.

---

[1] You have never understood anything in life. And now you start messing me about in my work.

[2] I repeat, what I have always said. If those Slavs stayed at home, it would be better for all of us.

Slowly Katharina followed the boy with the broad shoulders. This is what she herself called him; she did not know his name and had no desire to find out. Her slight figure was totally concealed by those shoulders.

A tacit relationship had established itself, and the silent or unspoken words bounced from one to the other like tennis balls on a disused court.

The streets were narrow and steep, first uphill, then suddenly downhill. The boy was walking slowly to allow her to follow him. His long legs advanced at a restrained pace, nevertheless it was a long stride for her and put her at a disadvantage. Every now and then she leaned on the metal rails used to brace oneself against the wind.

They had gone a long way and were not yet at the sea, it seemed as if it had pulled back and never touched that city. They were climbing gently, leaving behind the last nest of houses and long walls encircling divided cemeteries. Rays of cold light reflected from a tangled mass of metal pipes and beat against the window panes of the warehouses. Several panes were broken, dark squares of incurable decay. Wide, empty roads scarred the hill, and long stretches of stones and stubble were neverending. Beyond the gorges that led into the mountains, clouds appeared.

They had arrived. Down there, that long line drawn with a ruler, was the sea. Beyond the fields, divided and cut by crosses, the oil pipes stood up like prehistoric mouths. The line was perfect, as if the precision of the ruler had not foreseen any change of colour. But in spite of such perfection it was turning grey and the paralysed arms of the cranes were ready to gather the ash.

They found themselves in an abandoned building site. Its gate was secured by a rusty chain, the rubbish spilled out of neglected bins.

Katharina did not know how they ended up there. They were still silent. The boy did not seem to remember, and she did nothing to make him aware that she was there. She had only followed his steps; she was looking now in the same direction and found herself making the same small movements he was making. She stopped by the heap of abandoned bricks and took her shoe off. The damaged heel, caught in the grating, was bent and made her unsteady.

The boy had moved away, jumping over the crossed bars of the gate. She saw him drop down behind some heaps of stones and lime. She caught his eyes in the distance, it was the first time he had looked at her. She touched her face, down as far as her neck having the distinct impression that his look made her exist for a moment.

She was not curious to see what the boy was doing in that uncomfortable position, she could not make it out in any case.

Twilight emphasized the distance.

Memory could not recognize the place or the moment to stop. She felt a heavy weight on her head, as if it were being squashed by a strong hand in a green glove.

She did not like sunsets. Her eyesight would fade suddenly and remain weak until evening. Objects would take on peculiar forms. The contrast modified the relationships between shapes; every bright area would conceal those nearby; the contours would split into two and imaginary clear lines appear against the dark background; bright spots would cluster in constellations and because of the multiplying number of fires, the haloes of their rays would join together.

She had consulted doctors, uselessly. Last summer she was afraid . . . of being dazzled, not being able to see . . .

There were people in the square in the town of Split. One summer evening. A chattering of languages drowned out her own.

She touched an ancient column, longing for a distant silence; the marble was crossed by deep veins and in that network a dark core showed resistance.

She found herself thinking and speaking fragments of languages; in their tangles she felt an outsider. It was the same fear of blindness. "Words," she said. "I must find the words . . . they will not understand me."

She entered the surgery of a Serbian doctor. She spoke English though she knew Serbian. She felt the need of a precise language; her eyes could not see, and so she spoke English.

The doctor was standing in front of her, blocking the window. He was tall, much taller than herself. He was listening to the accumulation of words and shook his head rejecting them. Then he asked coldly:

"Jeli to prvi put da vam se dogodilo?"[1]

"I don't know," said Katharina in English. "I don't know. It seems now to happen more often. As summer approaches the pain comes back again and again. I wonder why?" And she sat down.

---

[1] Is it the first time that this has happened?

The stool was high, without a back. Hieroglyphs and vertical letters similar to one another moved up and down, at times becoming clearer, at times confused. Black, narrow and tall marks. Turning her gaze in a different direction she could modify their relationship. As if she were re-establishing contact with her body, she thought aloud:

"Imala sam strah uvek, jos kao devojcica, da u jednom trenutku ne bih videla vise . . . To je stari strah od mraka. Mozeti li me reci tagot? Ima nesto sto nikad nisam saznala ili mi nije receno, mozda nika porodicna bolest koia pogadja oci."[1]

She found it difficult to sit in the dark on that stool. The ray was probing into her pupils; a dot of cold light that grew larger and glowed, created roses, patterns, geometrical shapes like star-fish. It spread all around a halo of fine, straight, well-centred radiations. The doctor had dark, shiny eyes like Arabian mirrors.

Suddenly there was light in the room.

Those dark, still eyes looked at her. He bent his shoulders slightly forward as if to reach her and said:

"Vase oci su svetle, previse svetle. Vi to znate jel'te? To ste zna od uvek."[2]

Katharina nodded, took the doctor's hand and held it against her face. The words were slipping from her lips as if from an overfull container.

---

[1] "I have always been afraid, ever since I was a young girl, that suddenly I might not be able to see . . . It's an old fear of the dark. Can you tell me anything? Is there something I have never known or that has been held back from me, maybe a family illness that affects the eyes?"

[2] "It's only that your eyes are pale, too pale. You know, don't you? You have always known."

The next day Katharina returned to that bright room. The light was filtering through the low windows, resting on the sofa. A lamp behind the screen silhouetted crystal flowers with open petals. The flowers were swinging, gently suspended, and their perfect alignment gave a feeling of lightness. The furniture softened the outlines, a dark stain made the green wall hangings look heavier. She relaxed her body and eyes. In the semi-darkness gleams of thoughts appeared, the air was a dust of light and desire.

She shook herself and saw the boy nearby.

"Why didn't you want to look at the murdered woman?" he asked abruptly.

He had pounced upon her. She had expected neither the question nor his figure hidden behind the heap of bricks.

For a few days, since she had arrived in this city, she had felt as if her thoughts, threatened by everything, would vanish. She had the impression of not being able to see for long periods of time. "It's only seconds," the doctor had reassured her. But it could not have been seconds, because the boy had covered some distance from the place where he found himself, a hidden place behind the plaster which had turned to stone.

How long had it taken to move away from the place of the murdered Serbian girl to the building site? The fear of losing her eyesight at sunset must have been connected with that shadow that overwhelmed her. It was something which refused to take the shape of a thought, clung to her body and stunned her like the belly of a wave when it rises filled with sand before running and breaking.

"When did I see the Serbian girl?" she asked. "I do not remember seeing her. You prevented me, didn't you?"

"No," answered the boy, "I did not. I was in front of you when the stretcher went by. I helped you gather the things that had fallen from your bag, I still have the smeared photograph."

"Maybe it isn't mine," replied Katharina. "I never carry photographs, they always reflect different images from those when they were taken; that second is lost like light and shade."

"Listen," insisted the boy, "you are here in a city you don't know or haven't seen for a long time. I saw you before the murder. You were coming out from the milk bar where they didn't give you any milk; the concierges were passing comments on the crime and going on about Slav girls."

The boy added with a sad smile:

"I have a lot of time, too, whole days. I come to this building site. It's odd, but I always find someone here. There is an old man who waits for hours sitting on the lime. Here it's easy for me to talk." And he stretched out on the rough ground, speckled with yellowed grass.

Katharina noticed that his leather knapsack had holes in the corners; small coins were protruding which would soon fall out. She worried about it and warned him.

She turned to look at where they had slowly climbed along the side of the hill. The roofs of the houses by the sea seemed to her closer, just beneath them.

"Clearly we shall not go back that way," she thought and said:

"I would like to be in town before nightfall. But don't worry, I do not want you to accompany me. Tell me the way or draw it here. Near me it is dusty, but where you have your knapsack the hardened lime has had its surface worn to a whitish film. You see, we can draw there."

She picked up a large, rusty nail and demonstrated how she could scratch the ground. Then she smoothed it with the back of her hand, picked up a long root which lay across the patch and threw it far away.

"Why don't you carry a pen with you?" she asked, and, smiling not to annoy him, continued:

"For goodness' sake, you are all the same, but think you are different. You think that you can keep everything as if in a safe, but the cells will crumble for you, too. We mustn't talk . . . for you it is all useless, silence. You scorn any sign and we go on decoding a mere nothing. Will you not grant us a moment? Maybe that wall will fall down, what do you think?"

"You are saying these things and hiding some thoughts," remarked the young man, and the liveliness in his voice lessened the distance between them. "You feel offended if we do not talk to you; you don't know silence any longer. You have chatted a lot and silence is a burden to you. But I like you."

"How old do you think the girl was?" asked Katharina, following an inner thought.

"I don't know. I think I heard people say she was twenty."

"I don't understand that murder," she said, "but, perhaps it is this city I do not understand; it has always been difficult to follow its streets, all its races which mix their tongues."

The boy was not listening to her last words, he was looking for something to fix her heel. She called out to him:

"It doesn't matter if the shoe is unstable. I shall find a cobbler near the coffee bar."

He came close to her. He was holding a mongrel puppy; one could see at once its throbbing, its heartbeat was fast and convulsive; he gave it to her without saying a word. "To act without saying a word is this boy's main characteristic," she persuaded herself.

She received the throbbing parcel from the boy's arms, almost frightened by its frenzied tremors. She put it down gently near the bricks. She followed its awkward and irregular pace. It was walking sideways, without direction, its legs were still having difficulty in supporting it. She was struck by the dismay and innate sadness in its moist eyes.

"You can keep it," said the boy with a certain harshness compensating for a sudden catch of emotion in his voice. "I can't, where I live they do not want anything, not even a little bird. You see, one day I found the cage that I had put it in open. As you know, if the birds can't fly they fall, don't they?" In speaking these words his voice trembled. He had the red face of a boy angry at an injustice.

Nothing came to her lips, she could not make even the smallest gesture. She had remained still, sitting on the hard, darkened bricks. She felt a stone prick her thigh, and realized that she had not noticed it before, that sharp point which was determined to pierce her flesh and which her hands and nails could not restrain. She tried to move her lips but felt embarrassed at the idea of not being able to take care of that little creature. She was sorry to hurt the boy. He had moved away and was trying to mend the heel of her shoe.

"We could take it somewhere," she decided, gathering the words with hesitation. Her voice was almost guttural, with the forgotten inflections of a foreign language. "But I cannot even recognize the city. I am here only for a few days. I am waiting for a person who should have been here already."

"In this city?" asked the boy, handing over the shoe with the heel still wobbling. "A strange city for an appointment."

"It is the sea's fault," said Katharina. "The sea, you know, takes people away from us, and they simply forget to come back."

"Yes," said the boy. "Mother was the first to go. I don't know whose fault it was. I have not seen them since, and if my mother comes back . . ."

"Haven't you thought," she asked, "that perhaps nobody showed affection towards her?"

"That has nothing to do with me," muttered the boy. "She should have known that." He gave a pull to the already frayed belt of his knapsack.

"We'll find a solution," she added. "Let me see what you keep in your knapsack. I am curious to see what you put inside these bags."

"I don't own anything," said the boy. "There is an old Greek exercise book, I like that language, I'd like to see Greece. Oh, yes, I have some telephone tokens, I am afraid to be left without any. And also grandmother always gives me pills for my headache."

"There is no longer any need to draw me the return route. I know it. I remember it now," she said firmly. "And in any case we are going back together." She took off her dark glasses and looked at the boy with her naked eyes. His eyes were too blue; it was rare to see eyes like that, of such a colour, blue and round, two buttons of precious glass.

It was getting dark now. Behind the building site

shadows fled, others lingered insistently. The darkness marked the distances.

Katharina rubbed her eyes unthinkingly; perhaps an eyelash irritated her, or maybe the light breeze.

A thin fog covered the outlines of things, everything dissolved in shade and silence.

The dampness was thick. She touched her hair which hung heavy on her shoulders. Something different to anything she knew kept her on that heap of bricks. Her hands rummaged through the little, grey gravel stones; she was looking for words and her mind had sudden unexpected sparks and incoherent thoughts. The puppy bouncing before her had a similar difficulty in co-ordinating emotions and movements. There was a break between her mind and her motionless body and little by little she gave up the struggle.

The boy was waiting motionless. The mongrel puppy was now resting drowsily in his arms; it was sleeping curled up on the boy's pullover and, while dreaming, its hind legs made quick jerks. "It's only a slight myoclonus,[1] puppies cannot dream." And she took it back so as not to disturb its sleep. The boy put on his rust-coloured pullover without shaking it. It was still warm.

His expectation that she would speak and move paralysed her. Her voice did not belong to her, it was the hoarse sound of an instrument worn out by neglect.

"I would like to find it," she heard her voice as clear as water. "Yes, I would like to find the violin again."

In the grey mud of the path that led to the gate, the colours of sunset merged together softly.

---

[1] Quick muscular contractions which occur during certain phases of sleep.

They started walking down along the short cut, looking among the white, pointed stones that pressed through the reddish tufts of grass. The boy preceded her, jumping down and leaping over the stones.

"What a strange earth," she said aloud.

"What are you saying?" he shouted in his turn.

"What a strange earth ours is," she corrected herself.

They went down another steep short cut. The damp leaves were rustling, water only just below the surface was seeping away towards the sea.

While descending she had the impression that the sky was rolling itself up and that the last blue of the evening was impregnable. She stopped for a second. She could not see the boy, but he came out of a reddish cluster of shrubs. "It's the light," she noticed with surprise she had never observed it with such attention. "It's the effect of the light which sinks into darkness."

A few lamps were lighting up, flickering in the early wind.

The smell of the season gave her a different vitality, energy of the summer heat, impetuous yet restrained.

She was walking past scattered lamp posts. As a young girl she would clench her fists to restrain herself from the wish to touch the wires. She would look at the white skull painted on the pole, horrified by the emptiness of the eyes, and would immediately touch her own.

"I am afraid of blindness," she cried out. She picked up a stone and threw it against a pole. It made a dull noise, yet it was an area where stones had echoed from time immemorial.

The boy pretended to be observing some bushes in order to wait for her, so as not to be too far away from her during their descent. He shouted at her as if he had known her for ever:

"I am going down, don't worry. I only wanted to show you this way. There is a track marked by the Slav peasant women when they come to the market."

She received his voice in silence, a rustling of birds about to leave. The puppy slept on against her breast.

"Wait for me," she shouted to the boy. "There is something more than a building site down there."

"But down there is the border."

"We can give it to the custom officers, they will probably have some milk for the puppy. Then, somebody will take it home."

"It doesn't matter, I'll keep it," concluded the boy. "I'll take it to school with me in the morning. That way, where I live they won't see it much and will get used to it." He came close to her and in a gentle tone added, as if talking to himself: "Tomorrow I shall go fishing for eels, if you like you can come as well."

"I don't like eels," she answered, "they are too slippery, how can you catch them?" And added, "But I would like to watch you."

The houses were grey in that part of the city, low and grey. The lighting looked strange, the street lamps were shrouded in a phosphorescent glimmer.

The road sloped and narrowed, it did not seem to her that she had passed along it before. "I would have noticed the slope," she told herself. It was hard to walk on the road or on that narrow and uneven pavement. She made for the road.

Only a few cars went by, slipping away in a hurry, appearing to be vehicles without drivers. From a little van some goods, probably unsold stock, were being unloaded into a dark entrance. Passers-by made their way stealthily into taverns which gave out hot, stale air.

Her watch had stopped at a time undoubtedly different from the correct one. Maybe that was the time. With a simple calculation, she could work it out. The light had faded slowly after the murder of the Serbian girl.

The boy was walking only a short distance in front of her but it was enough for passers-by to believe that they were not together.

It was a form of security and she quickened her pace. A woman coming out from the tavern knocked against her; a known face, the cheek bones came back to mind when she saw her. The woman tried to ask her for something, but she turned away indifferent to those remembered eyes.

The smell of wine was escaping from the entrance hall, it was stronger than usual, and was coming from a large puddle, spilt but not cleaned up. She hurried on, feeling sick. Her voice died in her throat. She tried to call out for the boy who was increasing his distance. She realized she did not know his name, and did not attempt to ask.

At the bottom of the stairs she saw again the body turned over and noticed a disgusting smell of acid. Dark, flat fragments similar to broken sections of mother of vinegar were floating at the bottom of the bottle, like fish long dead.

She dipped her little finger, white like wax, in the spilt wine that was quickly running away along the pebbles. She attempted to write her son's name on the cold stone. Despite her best efforts she did not succeed. "When was he born?" she still heard the man asking her from the other side of the glass. "When? Who?" she had said, and moving away from the wax head and from the glass she had sat down on the wooden bench in the school hall, waiting.

4

A fine rain was falling gently on the people walking aimlessly along the avenue. Sodden leaves were falling from the trees and piling up. Lazy dustmen had left that rust-coloured mush believing that the rain was making their work pointless.

Few people remained seated in the open. The coffee bar, although sheltered, was almost deserted. The crowd drifted away and the colours were like sparks for her mind.

All of a sudden the small, sleepy orchestra in the corner of the coffee bar reawoke. The players, whom Katharina had just before observed with satisfaction for their silence and curiously relaxed postures, clung to their instruments as if to support their bodies.

The semi-darkness with its colourless shapes and faces was urging that solitary company to escape. Suddenly, as if waking up from a torpor and obeying an order from outside, they made abrupt, uncoordinated movements and struck up a waltz. The accelerated rhythm of the notes accentuated a vulgarity the composer had not intended.

She dropped the newspaper and the wooden stick fell against the marble of the coffee table. The disturbance was so strong that it put an end to the anaesthetized attitudes of a short time before. She was submerged by the screech of the violins and the flutes; the bassoon was croaking painfully. The irritation grew to the point of fear, her head was hurting and the blood was pulsating at her temples. "Horrible octaves of an unbearable music."

"What's happening to me? Am I thinking aloud?" And lifting her eyes from the newspaper, among the black figures huddled in the chairs, she saw a man at the table next to her, so close that she was affected by the annoyance in his eyes.

"You, too, are in flight from octaves in life?"

She felt the reason for her irritation with the players' octaves was their insistence on distinguishing between consonances and dissonances.

"No," she answered, "I am not running away from octaves . . . only I would like to hear the shades of the harmonics higher up."

"In this place," added the man, "it is always the same . . . They play the music devoid of any feeling, they assimilate different motifs, Maria Theresia and the Emperor Franz . . . Believe me, it would have been better if they had never played." He said this looking at her carefully. Katharina noticed his voice before even seeing his face. It was a deep, caressing voice; it gave the impression that the words remained in the air suspended by a very long thread.

"Like in dreams," she thought, "when someone calls from far away and you run to get closer. The voice runs after you and in hurrying towards the call, you hear it further away from where you thought it was originally; and you don't know which way to pursue it; you do not know where it is coming from and what it is saying to you. The text is lost in the air like fine sand and you do not wish to return to see and to listen."

"You like music. Well, through the notes one builds

an architecture. One effect must be just so because it connects with another effect; emotion lies elsewhere."

"Yet," Katharina replied, "harmony is a law of sound which does not embrace the physical order alone. It is a world which vibrates with the feelings that move within us."

"It seems that the help of the mathematicians has been essential," admitted the man, "in order to understand how harmony unites the structures of things, different situations and meanings."

Katharina picked up the newspaper from the floor. The man no longer doing anything to interrupt the train of her thoughts.

"Maybe they have stopped playing waltzes for today."

"Are you Serbian?"

"I'll be here only a few days," she limited herself to saying.

"Only a few days?" said the man, and seemed to be speaking to himself more than to her. Without waiting for an answer he decided: "Let's go into that empty room inside, it's beginning to get cold here."

She did not answer but accepted with relief. She wanted to keep listening to those brisk words.

"I do not know you and you do not know me," continued the man. "I don't care about names. They do not mean anything. I am here drinking cold white wine with you and that pleases me." He looked her in the eyes, perhaps with the precise intention of producing the first rift in their instinctive relationship.

They had entered the deserted room. She felt colder but made nothing of it. The man sat next to her. She could feel his breathing. She looked instantly at his hands and had the idea that they were detached from his body. "They must belong to another man." And she replied:

"I am not interested in names either, and don't remember them, they are like numbers."

She saw him get up, reach towards the coat rack. She noted with relief that he was tall. He was wearing a corduroy jacket with broad ribbing, but it was too tight for him and sitting down he unbuttoned it, just as if he had known her for a long time. Fixing her eyes on him, she drank her cold, white wine.

She looked outside. The members of the orchestra were bustling carelessly about their instruments. The room was so badly lit that it seemed dark. She could see the movements of people nearby. "How pointless the gestures of the dancers would be if one saw them from a distance without hearing the music." And she thought: "Names are pointless and yet at times they define life, marking an importance where one does not exist."

She took off her dark glasses and put them in their case, slowly. She never did this, and so the lenses were always scratched. She was hiding the silence with what were for her unusual actions.

The room was almost dark. This annoyed her as much as the light. Her eyes reacted in the same way with slow and frequent twitches of the eyelids.

The man was not looking at her. He was drinking his wine in small, repeated sips. He was holding the glass with both hands, so she could observe them better. They were beautiful, in the semi-darkness they seemed to be wearing gloves made of smooth, slippery silk, like transparent rubber. The thumb on his right hand made some movements and was different, longer than normal, it moved up and down independently of the other fingers. In coming to terms with the body, through the delicate experience of the sensitive cells which activate movement, that thumb must have acquired a nerve of its own; it was beating in unison with the others and at the same time dominated all the sequences. Maybe the idea of seeing the body as an object, while nevertheless sharing its emotions, had started as an irritation around the foetus. She was drawn towards that almost irrational movement, took pleasure in it.

The man returned to an interrupted thought and said abruptly, almost to forestall any objection:

"Music follows a grammar of its own, it cannot reflect shifts of feeling. How could the discords, the voids be explained otherwise?"

"But the most hidden fantasies," replied Katharina, picking up the indecision of his question, "do they not answer a music score which allows . . . I don't know . . . infinite variations on a theme? The same logic is concealed in the mountains near here. You see. Their divided strata demonstrate a disturbed order, but the broken lines can be reassembled."

As if removing an uneasy feeling, the man continued:

"Tension unites . . . it does not weaken because each shape is not resolved. Pleasing sensations are repeated and new ones sought . . . This suffering does not abandon the score, it tunes the instruments. The score can then be forgotten, what matters is the motif itself that animates and organizes it without describing anything but the effort, its permanent unfinished state."

"Even the streams that come down from these mountains are continuous lines. Then they break up, they disappear, and they return with their distinctive strength or are scattered in playful games where every leap represents a new sound."

"New sounds can be produced."

"Just as chemistry produces new compounds which do not exist in nature."

"That is what is attractive, the bringing together of something which is dispersing. Each time the orchestra plays is an experiment. Overtures are repeated . . . one looks for the secret of a movement, openings are always imperceptibly different. It's the only history of which I can indicate the period. The players are intentions which are looking for each other. Mistakes are important, a perfect performance would be unbearable."

The glass was empty. She wanted the man to fill it, but he did not. Katharina kept looking at that thumb, it really seemed detached from the hand in the semi-darkness. Her throat was dry. It was as if another day had passed, distant in time from when they were sitting at the table outside and people were going by.

A waiter in a black jacket appeared at the door balancing a tray. He tried to turn on the light switch, but this hit the ground like a bullet and disappeared into a dark corner. Pirouetting like a circus acrobat, the waiter turned round keeping the tray intact. And the room remained silent in the absence of light from the large, useless chandelier.

With the minute concentration of someone who has plenty of time to spare, she shifted her observation from his hands to his face. She felt reassured; she seemed to know many things about him.

"But," she reflected, "the voice, the hands, the face of people might be what they have become, not what they were." Then she amused herself guessing which and how many traces had affected her, which ones had slipped away like rain, which ones had stuck . . . traces, traces gathered in a bundle . . . on that impenetrable face.

She might have already seen or met him before, but

had not. Yet, she had to find that face in her life. She tried to go back to the beginning; examined the grain of his skin. "The colour deceives," and she wondered, "maybe he is only pale after an illness."

With that man everything was possible and, at the same time, impossible. She analysed the parts which could form a person and found it difficult to combine them. She focused on the mouth and thought it was beautiful. But when his lips moved they revealed regular teeth, as sharp as razors.

"Yes," said the man, sensing that attention, "around me there is emptiness. I am alone."

"And the musicians, then?" asked her already distant voice.

"I left them some time ago . . . Their passion for underlining things and looking into things. How wretched! . . . They will never succeed in anything. Their chatter, words, pieces of froth which pollute a clear stream."

"There is froth also in this wine we are drinking," she reflected.

The waiters were making useless noises, dragging the tables along the floor. Some of them cast furtive glances into the empty room.

Quickly, the figure of the man got up. He was the only bright point in the dark room.

"We really must go, now," he said abruptly.

She saw him put his clenched fingers into the pocket of his large overcoat. He took out some crumpled banknotes, mixed with visiting cards. Without looking, he placed them near the empty bottle. Some fell and Katharina carefully picked them up.

Her need to drink increased, but she allowed herself only to place her open right hand against her throat and swallow saliva. She adjusted the leather strap on her shoulder and followed him.

They were walking fast. The afternoon rain had given way to wind. It skimmed along the walls of the houses, not strong yet, it was only the beginning of the season in which it would be the leading player. Katharina could feel it beat against her back like a large fan.

The man was walking in front of her and his tall figure seemed to grow and shrink taking shapes with the wind. His large overcoat played with the breeze, assumed strange forms. He seemed not to notice the breathless figure who was trying to keep up with him.

They found themselves on the road climbing upward. She ran close to him and with her hand on her mouth because of the burning in her throat, almost shouted against the wind: "Here this morning a crime was committed. She was only twenty."

She had succeeded in grabbing the sleeve of his overcoat, and quickly twisted it in her fingers. He did not stop, only nodded with his head. His hair covered her forehead and his look rested on her shoes with such intensity that she looked at them as if their tips had eyes.

"On this side," said the man, "the road climbs a little, but it is shorter. We must go away from the sea."

"But I have only glimpsed the sea since I arrived . . . and also . . . I must go back to the hotel, I must, you understand . . . I am waiting for a message. It's late, but it will come. The hotel staff has just recently changed," she pointed out, "and Leopold is ill. You know Leopold don't you?" And as if he had reassured her, she continued:

"I have known him for a long time. The young man who is replacing him doesn't answer, maybe he forgets to write down the messages. Until Leopold comes back it is useless to wait for news."

They had moved away from the street and the coffee bar.

Darkness lay in the alleys. There were no more trees, and everything was locked as if it were late at night. It was only evening. Here and there a streetlamp stretched out its livid light onto the street, like a curved nose bent towards the mouth.

"I live in a back street not far from here," said the man. "It is one of the streets that leads to Piazzetta dei Trauner and to the old city gate."

"Yes, yes," she muttered to herself, "now I know where I am. The ancient gate. When I was a child I was told: 'if you go in, it will shut from the outside and won't open again until dawn. So you'll have all the gloom there inside.'" Instead, in a slow voice, lifting her arm as a sign of approval, she said, "I was there many years ago. Is the fountain still there just behind the gate?"

Her voice was like fresh water, the words turning into questions which stayed empty in the cold air. And the wind was repelling her.

"Wait!" She shouted. "The wind makes my eyes burn. Wait. Behind the gate was the fountain. It was there that the children gathered and splashed one another. Then they would wash their hands before going home."

The man had stopped not far away. He raised his hand slowly to cover his forehead and, with the thumb and first finger, half closed his eyes.

"No, now there is a little theatre," he continued, leaning his head against her arm; and Katharina noticed the high forehead marked by thin wrinkles. "Once on the mountains, I found fine writing like that buried in the desert." But these lines, she thought, were attached to a nose, to a strange curved item, and from the mouth came a smile.

They had climbed above the area of the dockyards. She glimpsed the wall of the church of San Giacomo and the street lamps close by the sea. Everything was centred in the area round that church: it was there that people gathered. She smiled, thinking back to old political debates; when she listened to them as a child she seemed to be in a puppet theatre where she was the most important spectator.

She searched for something in her bag and stopped, determined. She no longer cared about what he would do or say, she had suddenly become physically tired. She did not find anything in her bag that might hold her attention.

Behind the outline of the overcoat she saw again the shadow of the man; he had stopped by an entrance which in the dark seemed long and narrow. It was not a side door. With surprise she realized she had come a long way and that, having left the old houses, she was now in a different, or possibly just new, quarter of the city.

The man waited for her and, without speaking, pointed out the alley to follow.

They were going down. It was a garage. Katharina asked nothing, she could not have spoken to him. She was surprised to see him busy looking for keys, surprised that he could have any.

She had thought she would enter those rooms casually, as if into a coffee bar.

A few, scattered cars sat in the allotted spaces, empty, disciplined bodies. In the semi-darkness they appeared like splashes of varnish spilt and suddenly hardened, to which the dim light had given form and colour.

5

They left the empty space, and between the cars placed like splashes of hardened colour, climbed a short, narrowing iron staircase. The steps widened and, through a network of pipes still painted orange, they found themselves before a steel wall in which three lifts were visible.

They were close to each other. She noticed his smell. She turned her head abruptly, as when one looks at someone for the first time. The man took off his dark glasses.

He pressed one of the buttons. Languidly, she did the same without thinking. The man stopped her, holding her by the wrist, and said in a low voice:

"That one is slow and goes somewhere totally different, on the opposite side of the floor."

Katharina burst out laughing and, looking at him, asked:

"So, are we in a station?"

The man seemed not to notice the question and replaced the keys in the pocket of his overcoat.

The lift came straight away.

It was a fast ascent, at least it seemed so to her. The silence weighed heavily. The metal box expanded the emptiness and the absence of words was becoming unbearable.

She tried to form some phrases, so useless that they

died before being born, such as 'how many minutes do you have to wait for the lift at peak hours', or: 'tomorrow the wind threatens to become stronger'. The banality of the words disheartened her but had the effect of distracting her from the dullness.

As a girl she had learnt to say properly: 'Ich freue mich Sie kennenzulernen, Meine Mutter ist nicht da, doch sie kommt bald zurück.'[1] She could repeat these phrases at the top of her voice. But she did not utter them. The words battered against the frozen glass, she could hardly keep them in.

Hours had passed. Together they had felt the thin afternoon rain and shivered in the dampness of the open-air café. It had grown dark and they had drunk cold wine in the deserted lounge listening to the violins of a clumsy band. And they had left the café and the wide avenue behind, walking some distance on the semi-dark roads, crossing empty alleys. They had let the first wind of the season play a subtle game.

Now they found themselves in that steel box, immersed in a silence with no escape other than into a red-eyed emptiness.

The automatic doors opened onto a desert of soundless walls. Four closed doors. Within those few square metres an armchair of coloured plastic.

Katharina heard the whining of a dog behind a door. Music came out as delicate as the rain in March. "Is it Mozart?" she wondered, *"per questa bella mano"*. The

---

[1] I am pleased to meet you. My mother is not here, but she will return soon.

minuet quickened, she saw the softly stepping, long white stockings draw an invisible circle on the green carpet. The powdered heads made sudden, precise and perfect movements, as did the jewelled hands.

She felt the touch of blue velvet on smooth skin, the gentle difference in temperature between different parts of the body and the clothes. The villas slept in the dawn and the stone windows had their shutters closed. Their whiteness glittered within the layers of mist, a distinct thought suspended between nightmares.

All of a sudden, as if that silence had reached a critical point, the air seemed to coagulate, then shattered into petals that slid glittering along the bright wall. A quick decomposition, the dust producing unforeseen transparencies. In that pause looks became worried again and a sense of threat spread in the atmosphere.

The search for the keys seemed to her endless. She felt cold at the ankles.

The front door opened. The man stopped for a second at the threshold, still in his overcoat; he kept his hands in his pockets, both of them, and seemed without arms. He looked pale, tired. She looked at him properly for the first time. As he was. Perhaps, just a man.

She stood standing on the opposite side of the wall; gave a sharp blow with her glove. The spider fell without blood. Just one more test.

There were two rooms. Beyond the window a bizarre architect had erected something similar to a control tower. Ramifications of unending wires crossed each other, rootless trees were drawing occult messages in the night sky. The wind shook them, took apart the numbers of the code, and reduced them to slim, senseless subtitles.

At regular and repeated intervals dark windows lit up and became dark again. Down below, on the smooth asphalt, headlights shone phosphorescent, coloured like butter-flies, and like them they dived to the ground stunned by the impact.

"We have been away for a long time," he said. "My name is Bertrand Smoleck. I am from Berlin. I am sleeping here, but tomorrow I'll be somewhere else . . . another town . . . and it won't even have the sea."

He let himself drop into the worn chair. Its springs must have long since broken and he sank deeply into it. "Had there been a drum underneath," Katharina thought, "there would have been a boom."

The light revealed a colourless face. The man slowly joined his hands around his eyes to concentrate on those details that casual observation neglects or rejects. Thin lines wrinkled his cheeks and a crease wore its way from nose to mouth.

"I would like to fix the world through camera shots. I would not miss the connections between movements."

"It's true," she replied, "our images are always so out of focus and retain only the thread of our desires."

They stayed motionless in the half-dark room. The perspectives were scarcely shown by the light, drawn towards the window only to mix imperceptibly with the cubes of constructions nearby, in a reverberation of distant rays.

During the night, marked by a series of luminous points, draughts of air spread out, pressing against surroundings and surfaces. Smells and colours troubled barren desires, uncovered fears and shudders that troubled that aquarium-like luminescence.

Each moment the atmosphere became more dense, animated by particles that glittered from the window as if through a camera with torn bellows.

Through the window panes, that brought things closer like magnifying lenses, one could see pigeons walking along the eaves of the *Prefettura*[1] building. Strutting along, they stood out against the iron and the cement; some took flight and described circles, following patterns like desires. The room seemed to expand with the breath of those flights. It was too early to leave and the way back was uncertain. The piazza looked on in silence at wings which folded with a quiver.

"I have travelled a lot," Bertrand Smoleck said. "Often, when I was still a child, I would prepare a small suitcase, and inside I used to put two pairs of gloves, always the same ones."

"You did not know then that you would become a musician."

"No, I did not know it . . . I just enjoyed constructing roads that intersected. With different pebbles I used to fix the borders. You probably know that in the Bohemian mountains there are many different stones, of unusual varieties . . . Mixing languages has always been a game for me . . . I would find new and strange words, change meanings, make up accents, sounds . . . it was my crossword puzzle . . . I never think of a theme in any one language, I have the feeling that it would limit it . . . But it is not reality, Katharina, it is my illusion . . ."

"No," she replied, and wrapped the raincoat round her legs, "you are right, I too sometimes feel that thought is surrounded . . . like thick liquid at the bottom of a glass.

[1] A kind of police station. (Tr.)

This plays nasty tricks . . . It's like beating against the walls in dreams, they always vanish . . ."

"My dear Katharina, haven't they taught you that images remain, even if," he murmured, "they form stains that spread out at the edges like oil on silk."

"My God!" she exclaimed. "We do complicate our lives. And yet I am here for a precise purpose, I repeat it to myself for reassurance . . . I married a man, a day I cannot remember . . . and he keeps me far away from my son Friedrich, this is a precise purpose I imagine . . . I must meet with the lawyer who is late . . . for a banal reason . . . And I meet a musician from Berlin . . . everything returns and disappears or is absorbed . . . Yes, you put it well, like oil, but oil on a sponge."

Bertrand Smoleck did not look at her, he was far away, listening.

"As for helping you," he said, "I think it is impossible for me. Over me, too, there hangs a shadow . . . it covers the dearest ones . . . If really someone inside us could tell us our dreams."

"I would like to touch physically what happens to me . . . but the noise would remain . . . I'm afraid of its thickness . . . of being encircled . . . It was like this in the garden that enclosed me as a child . . . it had a high wall, damp and dark bricks, I did not go out . . . and the voices rose without my being able to see anything . . ."

Bertrand Smoleck was looking elsewhere. His profile was pale, his mouth half-closed, his eyelashes long and strange, like those of a child.

"Once in Prague, I had just finished a concert, I was exhausted. My mother had died a few hours earlier, they told me as soon as the concert was over. I thanked the audience, once, twice, I felt a pull at my right hand, my arm fell forwards unconnected. I felt a pain in my right eyelid and looked at the audience again, confused, as if I were there by chance. The audience had turned into a thick crowd with hands lifted not any longer to applaud me, but to shout at me . . . You see Katha," he resumed, "since then that crowd has not left me."

Katharina entered the space of his arms bending her head backward; so hard that she almost felt it detach from her body.

"You know Katha," and he brushed her neck, "my mother, too, used to wear a string of pearls like yours."

"It's all I have from that period."

Bertrand Smoleck's words were a distant sing-song:

"Ein altes Wiegenlied . . ."[1]

"I, too," Katharina whispered, "have walked without a reason . . . It's only one night, a few hours, but I am with you."

Something undefinable forced her down on the low divan. She listened to the silence, she was afraid that her breathing would shatter it. She tried different ways of breathing through her nose. She breathed through one nostril, then through the other. Like that her mouth could stay closed.

"I met a woman," he started again. "She had an appointment . . . but the details escaped her . . . The signs change . . . Now and then she chewed a white tablet."

"And discovered," Katharina asked, "the shortcuts, the crossroads of the old city?"

Bertrand Smoleck took off his glasses, they had left a

---

[1] An old lullaby.

clear mark at the top of his nose, almost a crack. He stroked his eyelids with his left hand, they were slightly swollen. He was looking at the point on the wall where the spider had been squashed and continued:

"Did you visit the monuments? They are isolated. They have an artificial location. The stones of the pier. The canal. The statues. The heaps of rope. This is what I like."

"Yes, I saw them and I, too, have noticed the distance . . . but one meets people, one speaks many languages."

"And one remains somewhere else."

"In exile?" Katharina added.

"No," Bertrand Smoleck replied, "carried by the movement of the sea. It's like in music. One resumes every motif, in order to understand its construction . . . and one gets entangled in a net . . . The game of languages and notes is the freedom of a fly in a jar to which it is attracted by honey."

"Something should take shape amongst these walls," she added, "architects have always taken trouble over defining a space. Once the façades were curved by the movement, science opened up unexplored dimensions and the lines stretched out in an endless development. Now they feel that certainty escapes them and look for rigour; they hate ornaments. They leave the interiors to the imagination of their inhabitants and are proud to regulate the outer structure."

"Here earlier than anywhere else," Bertrand Smoleck specified, "architects felt the need for empty spaces. Owners would foster a destiny behind the façades, each according to its own. Why restrict the development of commerce to a fixed figure? And hence these great spaces, beneath massive beams, waiting for the wheat and the crates."

"But the turmoil of the warehouses ruined the bright façades."

"Yes, and those underground spaces had the atmosphere of isolation wards, hospitals . . . There is a villa with a mysterious façade in the old part of the city . . ."

"One gets lost in that part of the city . . . it's deserted . . . and the gates rusted, the gardens with their tall grasses are almost the same in all the villas . . ."

"It's a house apart . . . it stands out, even if you wouldn't call it a hospital . . . large, old, along the ridge of the hill . . . the façade crouches behind the boundary walls, and in the walls terrifying eyes open up . . . So many inmates have lived behind those walls and their voices became hoarse like those of birds exhausted by the wind . . . and they all ended by sinking slowly, level by level . . . and it's strange . . . really strange . . . in order to get down they climbed the mountain, high up into the silence of empty orbits . . ."

"I have the feeling that I was once there . . . much time has passed."

"This city, with its bright façades, will descend into the darkness, the villas and the gardens . . . This city and you . . . you know only how to wait . . ."

"I know that one day I will follow the walls that hide the old grass, paradises that shine like frescoes under the sky. We will waken the white statues, on a languid afternoon."

Bertrand Smoleck stood before the window, his back towards her. No noise. The glass tower, with a shrug, had got rid of all its inhabitants. In that empty geometrical beehive only a man and a woman with their silence were not out of place.

"Now, I'm afraid," Katharina thought, and held her breath, "afraid of seeing him."

He became aware of her, turned suddenly. In his eyes was wonder at finding her.

He seemed ready to start conducting. Leaning forward, his feet bent and almost balancing on his toes. His hands were stretched out along his body, his whole face contracted, waiting. His nostrils breathed out, as if the air itself did not convince him, and they opened and closed in jerks like tailors' dummies. The skin on his face stretched out, taut on the cheek-bone.

"The eyes," Katharina gasped. "Two black clefts." She was being watched by him, she was sure, she could not move. "Is he afraid as well?" Something moved her. "Perhaps the auditorium will be empty tomorrow. And that tic in his jaws will bother him, his hands may betray him, a conspiracy behind his back."

"And the orchestra?" The word escaped her, impossible to take it back, it had rolled like the tennis ball of an absent- minded child against the empty wall.

He rested his profile on his left shoulder, towards an imagined violin, and stretched out his right arm towards her.

"Yes," Katharina thought, "he, too, is afraid." She moved to go towards him. His body blocked for a moment what light filtered through the window. Bertrand Smoleck smoothed his hand as if it were the baton. A cat would have fled under that sort of stroking.

She put her hand firmly on his arm and stopped it. Her voice came out clear, loud:

"You and your music," she shouted.

But he was not listening any more. His thoughts were

pursuing fantastic compositions executed by the waving palm of his hand. The room became his desert. "To advance into the firm sand, full of life, is that not to draw one's own geometry?" she thought, sharing the same desire.

His hands made violent jerks in empty space. And whilst the left one fell indifferently along the side of his body, almost touching it like the movement of a ballet-dancer, the right was raised, imposing and white, beating the thick air of the room to silence.

Now his body stood out against the large window, blotting out any illusion of light. Bright spots in the distance, like blazing firebrands in a storm, died in the night.

6

It was late morning, Katharina was thirsty. The glass stood empty on the chest of drawers opposite the divan. Something milky remained in the bottom and from a distance it looked like the sand in an hour-glass. "I would like to turn it over," she thought. But immobility was more reassuring and she remained lying down.

The window stretched the grey light beyond the door. There was a pale winter sun behind the drawn blind and the day was beating as if through a stage curtain.

She turned to look at the trail of light which skimmed the floor and lit up the dust, following it into dark corners where it became thick. She looked at her leather bag. Bertrand Smoleck had squashed it when he sat down, or rather when he sank into the chair, the night before. There was nothing fragile, she felt sure. The photograph could get damaged, but it was already worn. Or maybe the boy had forgotten to give it back? Had the boy not picked it up when it had fallen with the other things scattered on the ground near the murdered Serbian girl? "In any case it's too late."

She called out her own name twice, three times. Her name assumed strange proportions expanding through the empty room. She had nothing to say to herself, even less to answer. She only felt a vague discomfort because of that difficult name. As a child they had called her

"Očice",[1] to shorten the name and because her eyes were too large for her thin face.

"Očice, come here," her playmate would say to her, "bring your box with the glass buttons, we'll build new coloured streets." "How curious," she thought, "I can't remember his name." "But Očice," her friend scolded her, "you always have the same buttons. I don't want to play. Find some new ones. You have to take them, steal them, understand?" "From here?" asked the girl. "From the coats of your mother's friends. Otherwise I shall always leave you to play alone."

Her things remained on the floor. Slowly she had watched them slide off the chair, one by one. First the stockings, then the shiny petticoat. Only her jumper had remained, attached to the arm of the chair. She could have stopped the skirt falling, it would have been enough to put out a hand. She did not do it, it was difficult for her to think and at the same time have things to do.

She stretched out her leg, trying to find a restful position for her numb muscles. She did not succeed, her foot entangled itself in an odd way in the blanket, trapped in the only side that had become undone. The sheet had disappeared, maybe she hadn't even had one, yet she did not show the least curiosity.

She stretched out her hand across the empty space, and knew that she would withdraw it without having touched anything apart from the coarse blanket. She clenched her hand in a closed fist and drove her school-girl nails into her palm. She did not feel pain, she felt nothing.

---

[1] eyes (Tr.)

Bertrand Smoleck had left a closed suitcase behind the door to the little hallway, or perhaps it belonged to the previous guest. The overcoat, hung on the door-handle, was like an animal emptied of its innards. The light was spreading beyond the curtain and covered the coat implacably in the same way as a movie camera. Close-ups scrutinize the quality of the skin, altering its pores. This is what the light did to that forgotten overcoat; it erased the pattern, revealing its age.

Shivers ran down her spine. The blanket was insufficient for her. Without moving from the divan, she picked up some thick socks left on the floor and put them on. They were so large as to make her believe she no longer had feet.

The cold did not cease. She made herself deprive the door-handle of that shape that had become her only company. She put the overcoat on. "Now I'm a clown," she thought, "out of fashion, but still a clown." And she fell back onto the low divan.

She felt her ankles tied and for this constriction blamed Bertrand Smoleck's socks, so large that they stopped her from moving. She pulled them up better, with the same care that children use playing rabbits, when they put both feet into the same sock and jump.

Gone were the images of the squirrels. Yet, the colourful woods clinging to the red rocks were close by, and she could go back there. The Slav peasant women still came down amongst the rocks, carrying baskets on their heads.

She saw again the image of the woman walking by the glass door. Better than Leopold, she might have been able to tell her something, uncovering her bag with the coloured cards.

Her gaze rested on the telephone wire, dead. It was attached to the empty wall and on it indefinable insects had placed themselves among the dust. A spider moved away to find a different place.

"Has the telephone been cut off?" she had asked. "It was never connected," Bertrand Smoleck had replied, "and then . . . for a few days . . ." The hopeless wire crept across the floor like a dead snake. "There is always a snake with us," she had added, "and it shows the place where we should live." And she had insisted: "I could have called, to find out if Leopold is better." Bertrand Smoleck had not replied.

It was good coming back and seeing Leopold again. With his thin hand he used to give the keys to everyone, smiling. As when she returned to the house in winter, after school. It was one of those narrow blocks of flats along the sloping streets. The concierge chased after her every time, "no la xe mai finida co 'sti s'ciavi. Xe inutile lavar su e zò le scale."[1] But she had already passed the grey steps.

She rearranged the folds of the overcoat. She wanted to be alone, without being irritated by these folds. But her body showed disappointment, a warning where word and muscle tension were indistinguishable. And she rebelled.

"How can I explain to myself why I'm here? How did I arrive here?"

---

[1] It is never finished with these Slavs. It's a waste of time cleaning up and down these stairs.

It was an afternoon of fine drizzle along the tree-lined avenue. The chilled wine pleased her. It grew richer with the jagged colours which stood out from the images, recomposing the details of meticulous visits, conversations heard and repeated, fragments assimilated note by note.

The dialogues between the town and the country mouse needed to be rewritten because the ground was stony and the store-rooms were undisturbed below the brightly coloured houses. She had lived day by day, without future. Confident, like the country mouse, of surviving with a little yellow grass, where the shadow of blood surfaced and the olive trees had long been abandoned for the lure of trade.

"What could hunger ever do to me? At worst I can cut the paper into small pieces." The organ-grinder drew his music from simple paper strips accurately folded. "That's what I'll do, I will live off nothing, in this dull room which isn't mine."

During the night, getting up, she found nothing amongst Smoleck's things. The bathroom had been cleaned; in his bag there was the odd loose tabet.

"In any event I cannot go out," she concluded.

She stretched out her arm, took the jumper and put it over her eyes. As soon as it was dark, her eyes lost some of the soreness caused by wind and exhaustion.

She was climbing along the wall that flanked the Palace. Her nails scratched the stones, which rolled down one by one and gathered at her feet. The wall, as she kept close to it, quickly rose higher.

A dark carriage went by. Two tasselled horses were

pulling it. They were pawing the ground, rubbing their heads against one another. They were bleeding near the ear but they carried on stubbornly. The jolts made the carriage sway from side to side.

Katharina jumped onto the carriage step, but the female figure disappeared leaving behind her grey veil.

Meanwhile the horses freed themselves of their blinkers. She leapt into the driving seat, she knew where the reins were. That swaying would stop and she would return via the garden drive with the horses.

She was sure of it. The figure in the carriage was the woman she had been seeking for days, the woman with the unsteady gait, and the bag coloured with ribbons. "Tomorrow," she said, "I will see her again, at tea-time, in front of the mirror, beyond the glass doors."

The horses were young, maybe twins, and they carried on with their cruel game. She fell backwards, among the stones, on the white road. Her nose was bleeding. She did not have time to get back into the carriage. The figure inside pressed two fingers against the window.

The heavy iron gate closed again automatically like a lift.

On the other side of the road, walking backwards, Klaus appeared. He had the document bag tied around his waist and his arms were free. The first time, on the palm of his hand, he was holding a tray.

She could not stop the blood from her nose. The shoes of the horses had thrown up the stones. She could do nothing but wait for Klaus to arrive. He was upon her in a moment. The bag fell, the official papers slid around like torn leaves, covered in mud.

The blood marked instantly. The first to disappear was her son's name. She hardly had time to read "Friedrich entrusted to . . . the Juvenile Court . . ."

Rays of light traversed the night. Notes filled the air with sweet clarity. A large bright eye woke her from her pain and highlighted the relief of the façades as if they were organ pipes.

The windows on the building opposite sent back razor-like reflections. She tried again the game of placing her fingers on her eyes. The light still hurt.

Through the half-closed door water was slowly running away. That explained the smell she had been breathing for hours. She could not stand the humidity for long, it paralysed her breathing. Suddenly she became afraid of falling ill again. The oxygen bottle had been attached for days. Meanwhile the child had been born and was breathing also for her. Was it his, that long cry that she heard? Her life was floating in the void . . . this was like the lunar world we loved as children. She heard the cry of life stretched out as if in a tunnel.

She gazed at the plane trees again, the branches formed a formal arch, it was like being in a cathedral. Drowsy gardens followed one another, pampered like arrogant children. The houses behind the gardens were silent. She sensed their interiors coloured green and blue, she could see light filter through the blinds, leaving a long trail on the floor. She listened to the chatter, little bursts of short laughter. Children in white socks were savouring honey biscuits. She entered the avenue. The patients sitting on benches were strangely still and yet she could feel the weight of their looks on her neck and shoulders. A dark entrance hall received her and cold numbed her ankles.

The corridor was long and the doors all the same. A man dressed in grey spoke to her, he walked by her side beyond the glass door.

She waited in a corner. She asked nothing.

A black, faceless silhouette rustled up to her and gave her a white paper lined with blue streaks: yes . . . during the night some blood had coagulated and other blood had captured it.

A nun with an icy face, drawn skin and eyes too watery to seem hard, knocked against her arm. The report fell to the ground and she lifted up her head, surprised that a nun had not apologized. The nun turned round, her clothes gave off a strange smell, part medication and part something rotten. Katharina made a gesture of disgust and placed her hand on her hot face to protect her nose.

Behind the door people came and went.

She would never free herself from those figures, maybe she would destroy that shapeless thing inside her. Her nose started bleeding again. A big girl with a white apron passed hurriedly in front of her with some small bottles and gave her a wad of cotton wool.

She went out without turning. The fog had come down and there was nobody on the benches any longer. "Better like this," she said to herself. "They won't look at me."

It was difficult to return from the kingdom she had entered. The monsters blocked the road in front of Alcina's castle, and she would not risk raising her eyes toward the sun. In that kingdom images condensed, thick like the wet hair that weighed on her neck.

If only she could hear that cry of life again. And she still heard another cry, the one she had heard from Friedrich, later, when he took him away. It was a bright morning in March and dusk seemed never to fall. But it was not the same cry.

The tap must have filled the washbasin blocked by scale.

She shook herself out of the long torpor. The light was more distinct. The half-drawn curtain allowed a view of the tall building opposite, a glass expanse in which opaque lines of iron were visible. A clear sign of the times was in front of her, not impressive, yet sufficiently strong to make her wish to remain longer on the divan.

Lying down she had a better view of the corners of the sheets of glass.

The Viennese architect, in his understanding of people and of the city, had suggested that through that intact crystal surface the new might mingle with the old spontaneously. Light could penetrate the interiors freely. The sun, beating on the windows, would warm them in winter and heat would filter through the corners, even if the iron had been shaped by machines to perfection.

No more people. Far away, in the carefully worked filigree of pointed stones, remained the blurred images, the bent backs, the little, shuffling silhouettes. "All is well. The past is ours alone." The figures wrapped in blue could not lean out from these glass windows which skimmed the abyss like eyes from a summit and gathered the shifting reflection of the sky.

It was always skies, blue in spring, that the great architect contemplated. He had taught how to lose oneself in the atmosphere. Or were a few kilometres of air enough to make one forget Venice and the blown glass that got its life from the flames? From one of those windows cut with a diamond, perhaps the last one, somebody was watching the sea. On clear days, when the morning mist was broken up as if by magic, who knows if one could discern the lagoon.

The daylight increased, falling casually on the dishevelled divan.

Katharina did not have the conceit of their old dog who became annoyed when he could not make himself comfortable in his basket. The baby was little then and it was like this that she kept remembering him. She would find the baby and the dog again, if she got up and picked up the bag squashed the night before by Bertrand Smoleck. She knew the spot where that photograph had been taken, she could go there, but who knew if the low wall that Friedrich leant against was still standing.

The gates of the house had closed behind her with the speed of automatic doors. They only opened from the inside. In any case, she was outside and with no keys, they had never even considered giving them to her. She was always surprised when she saw people manoeuvring a bunch of keys, they seemed to her such different and important people.

With one hand she covered her face, but her eyes stayed open. She tried to spread her hand across like an open fan and her eyes continued to be open. The eyes of the dead stay open if somebody does not close them.

She had fled across the garden that night. She remembered the wind among the trees, a cry so human, which her memory had never since recalled.

"Leopold, you had done what was in your power. And then without you in the house, with whom could I have spoken our forgotten language?"

She could feel the humidity grow around her, and squeezed one nostril after the other to open them. Breathing was becoming difficult, so she opened her mouth to get more air.

She moved her body towards the closed door. A button that had come off Bertrand Smoleck's overcoat pressed against her breast.

She was in the right position and put her hands into the pockets of the coat. There was only a creased ticket from the Fenice theatre, they had staged *Iphigenia in Tauris*.

7

We sleep when our lids are lowered, our thoughts are then dreams.

The orchestra conductor half closes his eyes, yet still sees the musicians, follows them and leads them. Delicate veins web the darkness, thread their way among the notes, take shape, multiply themselves like figures gone mad.

There is a story with its roots in unexplored labyrinths, hedged over by a weft of deceptive branches. What a delicate touch the archaeologist must have who brings them to light; the ground reveals sudden hollows where bodies and matter dissolve, or else layers of darkness with minute differences.

Katharina directed her gaze beyond the shadow that engulfed her, and sought to penetrate its secret. She was close to grasping something. She was preparing for a way back on this unknown journey. She went through a mirror of water with floating images, but could not make out the stones and sand below at the bottom. She felt cold, her skin clammy. But it was not completely dark; a transparency shimmered in the water, a gleam. The room was divided by a reflection.

The fragments of that story danced before her like deformed puppets.

The room sank into semi-darkness. Only breathing broke the silence, filling it with particles.

A swirling network. In the laboratory filaments used to attract her. Behind the glass shone a black screen; one could perceive the slightest thickening. Words were drawn from the depths, a darkness which did not cover them, but made them visible. In the damp twilight thoughts sparkled, joined together, sank. Like clear, still liquids in flasks. She needed to stare at those particles from close to, since they would disintegrate like mercury and, when caught, were suddenly distant.

Of the morning rain, only drops remained on the hedge that enclosed the lawn. She had walked through the whole park, crossing it in every direction.

The certainty of the quadrangle forced her to move away. She would go as far as the gate, walk away from it, walk round. The noise of footsteps sounded like sighs over crushed leaves, the humidity made them crackle lightly. She walked with rounded shoulders. She felt a sharp pain at the nape of her neck and turned her head towards the tops of trees whose name she did not know. A ball was echoing, bounced by someone on the same spot. And always those same footsteps down there in the dust.

The nurse would come into the room. Big cheek-bones and a jutting forehead. The light was scant, she could not see her eyes. She would leave a white bottle on the cold bedside table, often bumping into the chair. "She does not speak," thought Katharina who would have liked to have heard her voice, but the other always left as soon as she moved her lips.

The shaft of light widened. Still those specks, a swarm where the shadow began. The floor was shiny, slippery. Her right hand felt cold. "Always the right hand," she thought, "in this heat this hand is cold." A tingling in her fingers, pin-pricks burned her numbed skin. Silence filled the room. She wanted to get out. "You are too weak." She knew it.

The sun was getting stronger. "It's afternoon already, the time of shadows . . . they reach across the wall and find the wrinkles in the paint."

Motionless, frightened by the slightest rustle, so removed from things, crouched in a single spot of her firm belly. Scattered shapes moved, reflected on the ceiling. A hot sweat was making her sticky. "It's different now . . . the shapes cross the threshold, are exposed in the shaft of light, stop on the floor. One could capture them. They have unsteady edges, the leaves waver, this movement spreads to the dust in the air."

"Take the book," he would say to her, "read it carefully." He prevented any possibility of her challenging his decision to leave her. And out he went. He would tell her to read some book or other and would not leave her free to wander in his absence. A book stood between them, and the written words that Katharina read in awe slid away like a cloud of particles in the shadow of the crack. "You see, it's like a town . . . to be totally discovered . . ." "Yes," she would answer quickly, and her eyes followed his gaze fixed on a point just above her head; he always stared beyond the boundary wall before going out.

"It's no good thinking about it." She rested her head against her knees. Her stomach was burning and her vision blurred, the heat beating under the skin of her temples. "He was curled up like this, tightly . . . when they tore him from my womb." She could see again the shadows under the door lengthening and reaching right up to her, covering her shoulders.

"But I really do love you," she was saying. She kept staring intently at his shoulders outlined against the window and observed his skin dappled by small patches of shadow. They were freckles, maybe, which the sun had made darker.

"I really must be going now," he was saying.

The deckchair was being unfolded. She heard the sharp snap of the wood and its support bar grinding in the gravel. The shadows were following her, the air outside was disturbed.

She altered the position of the deckchair. Now the dampness was making the shade opaque. The nurse came back, opened her hand, white particles were waiting for the palm of the other hand to open. A bitter taste in her throat. She wasn't given any water. "The water is in my mouth," thought Katharina.

She was falling asleep, or thought she was sleeping.

During the night she had not slept. Not a sound, nothing, and the heavy silence frightened her. Every so often she would put her hands over her ears just to feel a difference within that unbearable silence. When resistance ebbed, so as not to scream, she would grope her way out of bed and try to open the door which gave on to the garden. Night cloaked everything, even footsteps were impossible to retrace. She would anxiously try to find the hedge; something was confronting her, the rosebush with its amputated branches. "There will be some noise tomorrow," she reassured herself, "when I look for his footprints in the gravel."

The sun was shrinking the shadows at the end of the avenue.

He was approaching with a bundle of newspapers under his arm. She felt his gaze in her vacant mind. "Oh, Ines has mudded the day-time pills with the night ones again." A book was sliding against his linen shirt. It had a long title. "Structures . . . fragments . . . physics . . . in the language." "C'est la vision des nombres."

The park was deserted. No noise came from within, only broad swathes of dark and damp. "He is passing by near me . . . I can just see his eyes . . . it has always been difficult to look at his eyes . . . it's strange, it's as if I had never seen them before, they have a colour I cannot describe."

The deckchair alongside remained empty all afternoon; it was still open and he dropped the newspapers and the book into it. "Structures . . . fragments . . . ." Katharina strung the words of the title together, turning them over. She was remembering coming upon a formula, back in the physics lab when an element for completing the analysis was missing.

Inside it was darker still. Katharina peered over the back of the deckchair. She looked at the room. Nobody had turned the lights on.

The pullover had slipped down between the two chairs. He drew closer. She felt his breath. He had just shaved and when he bent down his face smelt of cologne. He picked up the pullover and gently laid it over her stomach. He didn't say anything, thinking she was asleep.

Her back was against the deckchair. He could not have put it anywhere except on her stomach.

In the car one day on that road shaded by birch trees, his hand resting lightly on the steering wheel . . . "I want your hand on my stomach." The car was stationary, a smudge of dark green beneath their bodies. "Your sweetness, don't take it away from me." "Hold me tight, down there, beyond the trees, it's dark already.'

She had thought that sleep might bring her some relief and that the monsters guarding her doorway would stir in that clear and silent water. She had found herself in a soft-walled tunnel and the light now annoyed her. Shadows busied themselves in broad daylight. The sun was coming in through the bare windows and was lighting that dreamless room, the streets noisy, the hotels now abandoned.

Nothing could hold back the quadrille of disjointed figures; she was fighting against those tireless and timeless images.

When old Leopold's sing-song ended, the lips moved with the tremor of senile paresis. Time had passed and the threats did not show, they followed the silence of odd mechanisms. When commerce had shaken off dependence on the Empire and the Slavs had become a guarantee for Franz Joseph, the people received their fifth curia, but this concession hid a plan. Now the Slavs could pass the border every evening and even the shadow of the master of regal tombs had withdrawn. In other suburbs he would meet youths to whom he gave money.

The bag was before her on the armchair, worn out through constant use. She could pick it up and enter the abyss of her imagination or the meanderings of the suburbs of a modern city. The hand of an assassin could strike anybody, it was pointless to worry. She walked a few steps on tiptoe. "Balance," she thought, "maybe it is not so difficult to achieve it." She was at one with the room. With her eyes closed she reached the chest of drawers and picked up the glass with milky dregs at the bottom. She brushed against the divan. The tips of her fingers were out of practice or maybe were still sleepy.

"You must go away," Leopold had whispered to her that night, "when the moment comes, be careful. I won't leave written messages, the boy who goes around with him would notice. I'll change the arrangement of the dry flowers in the Chinese vase. There are no flowers in the garden any longer, the man who looked after them hasn't come for a long time now. You'll go out through the garden door. It's dark there. That's what he wanted, even before his illness, his collections need shade. I'll look after the child. I've managed to find out where he keeps the key to the yellow room. Don't stay. The doctors said that. His illness will lead him to greater rages against you, against us, too. He won't notice your absence until late in the morning. Don't worry about me. Remember, the street in the old city, at number 9.

"As you know, your suitcases are locked away, it seems that not even he can get the room opened again. I have my little suitcase ready for you, the one I had when I first came here in service. You'll find it under the seat of the old carriage. I thought you'd be pleased to find inside it your child's coat with the astrakhan collar and the two jumpers that nanny knitted. The rest is all shut away.

"I'll leave the light on under the portico leading to the stable. It's a dim light. Don't bump into the loose planks, they've still got the old nails in them. There's too much stuff piled up.

"Remember, the dried flowers will be separated, in the red Chinese vase."

Leopold had not been able to say anything else to her. Along the corridor came the sound of dragging footsteps. Someone had been listening, or the wind had swung back one of the shutters of the windows overlooking the garden.

On the agreed night Leopold must have been stopped

or something must have interrupted his preparations. The clocks were all in the room with the showcases.

With difficulty Katharina left the long corridor which suddenly narrowed. Several times she bumped into the doorjambs. The corners of the chest of drawers were sharp, her right hip felt the bitter experience of them, and she had to kneel down and hold it with her hand so as not to scream. She found the rusty handle of the garden door and turned it gently, expecting its creaking to be even noisier in the dark and the silence. The door yielded. She did not feel any sense of contact, as though she were wearing gloves. She was in the open. She had expected the wind, but not the rain that was now beating straight into her face.

The portico had not been repaired for years, roof tiles were missing in several places. She waited a while, flattened against the wall. The light would come on in the stable. She realized that she was calling on the two religions which, confusedly, without going deeply into them, she had encountered as a little girl, and that she was thinking of that strange mercy to which Leopold turned. Help did not come.

The door that Leopold had advised her to use closed behind her from inside with a click. She had no alternative but to make her way past the heap of planks in the portico and to crouch down under the carriage. She groped around for the suitcase with the child's clothes, her hands fumbling. She found it by touch, right under the loose seat.

Her hands and breath steadied. "In the driving seat," she thought, "I'll find the rug." Holding the little case and the rug, she got down from the running-board of what had once been a fine carriage, but which she had never seen in use. She hid in its shelter.

At the attic window she saw a light go on and off two or three times. 'Maybe Leopold is telling me to stay." But the door had shut. She was outside once and for all.

The rain slackened off and the night was less dark, but the damp her permeated her coat. The rain had prevented Leopold from bringing the child.

The empty crate in which she was growing numb had a false bottom. The patter of the raindrops made her doze off. The blanket had retained all the familiar smells, particularly that of the old mare. She sneezed.

On the day when she saw her for the first time, the mare neighed loudly and shivered when she stroked her. "Why does she tremble like that?" she asked. "She's just old," he replied, "we'll have to think about it." He turned away from her at once, for as far as he was concerned the matter was over. A little way away, Leopold was moving sacks from the stable to the house. He was dropping things along the way without noticing it, and she ran to help him; it was enough to make him turn around abruptly and rebuke her. But she did not listen; it was the first of many such reactions.

Not long afterwards the mare began to have fevers. Then Leopold would forget at night to shut the garden door. Katharina would go out secretly to see it and cover it with the blanket which was now covering her.

One night, he noticed it. In the morning it was decided that the mare's illness could harm her in her state of pregnancy. And on one of those days, at dawn, when sleep becomes fluid and dreams slip out of focus like old photographs marked by dampness, she heard a shot. She opened her eyes. In the room nothing had changed, it was cold, very cold. She pulled up the duvet and covered herself. She turned her face towards the wall, solid like a pillar. She had made the wrong choice, even about that bedroom.

A weight pushed against her stomach, so hard she was afraid that it would pierce her.

She could hear nothing but Leopold's voice in the distance. She could not understand him, and yet he was speaking her language. The sound of his voice remained suspended in the air and the words dissolved.

Her belly had enlarged and its skin thinned like india paper. It was a drum that did not give out any sound. The scuffing of Leopold's sick feet became agitated. A broken shutter fell with a clatter. The door opened and a gust of wind blew open the window. The November leaves came in quickly, creeping furtively along the smooth floor, mixing with cotton wool soaked in a dark reddish colour.

A heavy hand weighed on her forehead for a moment, then held her hand tightly along the corridor with its whiter than white walls.

It was the wail of the siren that banished the last perplexities before dawn.

Hours went by in the room of Bertrand Smoleck. The idea that he might return to pick up the suitcase would confirm that her body had been touched during the night, that the coffee and the contorted dance band existed.

She would have liked to run through those streets again, to sit down again somewhere along the avenue.

During the night the rain had exhausted itself. There was a strange sun outside the window and she had to come to terms with that light. She would have preferred the rain. The dark glasses weren't there any more, perhaps she had left them on the table in the café next to the empty bottle. That room was deserted and dark, there was no need to shield her eyes, they were resting in the twilight.

She discovered a low fridge that she had not noticed before. It was behind a door left half open, which had hidden it. It was not even white like normal fridges. Somebody who had lived in the room for a long time had covered it in dark paper with a polka-dot pattern; it had come unstuck here and there. Its noise must have disturbed Bertrand Smoleck's train of thought, because the fridge was unplugged.

She opened it although she could guess what was inside it. The emptiness surprised her. In the salad box she found a tin of sardines of an expensive make. On the meat shelf two imported apples of an acid-green colour, hard and cold, they felt like marble. The mineral water was finished and the bottle had a mouldy deposit. In the butter compartment there was some *Schwarzbrot*. She touched the transparent paper, she touched the bread. "Seltsam, gerade das Brot, das ich am liebsten esse . . . also auch Bertrand Smoleck isst es."[1] She put it back, putting off the appointment: "Bis später."[2]

She could hear the water still running, on the other side of the door; it irritated her. She jumped up. She used to lift her head up like that as a child when they washed her hair; nobody had ever been able to convince her that she wouldn't suffocate.

---

[1] Strange, the very bread that I like best . . . so Bertrand Smoleck eats it too, then.

[2] So long.

The slow continuous dripping during the night had filled the washbasin. The water was overflowing.

She picked the clothes up off the floor. Her naked body bent over, her movements became quick. That stream of water was her burst dam.

She took the leather bag from the armchair. Her glance fell on Bertrand Smoleck's suitcase. She rested it on the only chest of drawers in the room. She noticed that it was empty; in one corner she could read an unknown name.

She closed the door behind her. She had not been given any keys.

8

She collided with an errand boy on a bicycle. His basket
with a bag in it fell to the ground. The paper ripped but
the bread was all right. Katharina, flustered, bent down to
pick it up. The boy bent down too, grinned at her, offered
her a brioche that was still hot. She took it, pleased: an
aroma of baking, of flour and jam blended in the heat.

"What will you do now?" she asked, "you'll have to go
back to the bakery. I can come with you and buy them
myself."

"Don't worry," replied the boy, "I always take a few
extra. I often bump into people. A few days ago I met a
foreigner. She was elegant. So are you."

"I must go," Katharina said firmly. "I really must."

"Come to the bakery one of these days," the boy called
to her, wheeling on his bicycle like an acrobat.

Then she felt like sitting down somewhere. She wanted
Bertrand Smoleck's words again.

Deep down in the coat pocket she had kept a little ball
of paper, the notes that he had left behind in the broken
wastepaper basket. On the creased paper his tiny and
fragmented writing had noted down: "Let's solve the
problem of time . . . the science scholar who tried to
understand his patients' perception of time ended up by
stopping with them."

Turning the corner of the street which she had walked along the evening before, she would come across the rehearsal room again. Perhaps, passing nearby, she might see him by chance. "But how does one look for an orchestra conductor when he is rehearsing? It's like calling out for someone who isn't there. It's like calling out for a dead child."

Anyway Bertrand Smoleck had gone. Maybe the concert was not even being held in that city. He was probably already in Berlin.

Katharina had slept for a long time, a deep, uneven sleep. Her tongue was swollen, she found it hard to swallow. "In the end," she said, almost aloud," I should have understood it. It is possible to understand even the difficult things." Now she missed Bertrand Smoleck.

She thought of his hands when he stood in front of the window, with his back to her. With a slow movement he made the blood drain from his fingers to his wrists, he did it furtively, an uneasy twitch, like a sudden fear.

The blood slowed down leaving his hands white and still as china ornaments. Then his back bent over the balcony rail into the darkness to look at the damp asphalt. It was a very tiring position. His arms moved jerkily, intermittently, they were conducting a different melody now, they hung away from the body like withered birch branches.

In the glass building some of the lights went out at the windows, like glow worms in early autumn.

"You know," he had told her, "you ought to look down into the street at night sometimes, in the cities where you happen to be . . . Du sollest es tun, Katharina."[1] As

---

[1] You really should do it, Katharina.

he turned round his dark countenance had an extra halo. Years had gone by in a flash. And he had stretched out his hands to her. She had done nothing in response to his gesture. Then, like a child whose mother has not cuddled it as desired, he abruptly withdrew his hands and pointed a finger toward the building opposite:

"The architect certainly hasn't produced aesthetic theories in the desert . . . Do you see, all the materials used are trying to seem better, or different from what they really are. Look, there, the whitened tin is dressing itself up as marble, the papier-mâché as rosewood, the chalk as stone, the glass as onyx. Somebody had to make the bitter assessment from the Secession: vanishing ideals which turned out to be tied to existing social structures. You know, a work of art comes into being without having to meet a real need. It wants to wrench men away from their comforts, that's why it's revolutionary."

Bertrand Smoleck had abruptly withdrawn his hand from her body. His features hardened:

"One can measure the culture of a country, a Viennese architect once said, by the amount of graffiti that cover the walls of its lavatories."

Now his expression was hard, as if he did not share the same room with her:

"Natural relationships have been turned upside down. It's the orchestra now that sounds the dominant notes, the singers are an adjunct. You want to decide whether some piece of music has a definite character? Then the only music you can take into consideration is instrumental music."

Katharina, letting go of his hands and wanting to extend the thread of thoughts and voices, had asked:

"Doesn't a certain connection exist between music and emotions? Isn't that one of the aesthetic canons?"

Bertrand Smoleck had withdrawn his hands. They were so white that they could kill, they were white like the body of the Serbian girl. But they would still have kept up their innocent circling movements, directing, mastering. Then, maybe they might warm up a little.

Katharina walked past the entrance several times. The smells that wafted out to her recalled others.

As she lowered her eyes to the ground and compressed her lips to avoid contamination, she noticed that just nearby there was a little low door. It was a little shop selling eggs and wine, so the sign said.

She slipped in furtively, and her pinched lips opened to respond to a welcoming smile.

The woman was wearing a skirt with deep, flat pleats like those of regional costumes, a starched egg-coloured blouse buttoned right up to the throat. Over the tiny little pearl buttons shone an oval locket, slightly out of focus, it probably contained an old photograph. Her little hands wore rings of yellow gold, trapped there for years and rather hidden by the swollen fingers. It would have been a difficult job even for a goldsmith to clear that space of the many things that had been put there and left. By some trick of proportion her hairstyle made her smile seem wider; the plaits rounded out her small head. On her feet she had cloth slippers which indicated a particular region, Katharina couldn't remember which. Her small feet could not easily have found suitable footwear, even if they hadn't been constricted by bandages. She moved in a youthful, nimble manner, yet it was hard to guess her age.

That windowless room was her shop. The woman served wine in small light-blue glasses, edged with thin dark-blue rims. They were made of ordinary glass and yet Katharina had not expected anything like that. She

felt as if she was drinking some elixir rather than wine.
White eggs were piled in a wide basket with a doughnut-
shaped cushion underneath.

Only the little low door, which gave straight on to the
narrow street, stopped it all from seeming an illusion. It
was like finding yourself on a papier-mâché stage-set, left
behind by travelling players. Nobody now knew what the
parts were and the script had to be reinvented. Was there
not once a little theatre behind Portizza? Perhaps, by kind
permission of the small woman, a first act was being tried
out. And the windowless room was the setting for the
interval, with the tired actors unable to taste anything
except an elixir of wine with a hint of egg in it.

Beside the door two small oval tables jostled each
other. A narrow bench, pressed against the counter,
peeked at the street. Bowls were filled with coloured balls
of fluffy wool, mixed with greenery.

Katharina kept silent, as when one finds just the right
position and is afraid that at the smallest breath the duvet
might shift its warmth elsewhere. She was in the habit
of forgetting her watch, but guessed that it must be
afternoon.

The woman, understanding what she wanted, did not
move. She simply transferred some meat balls from the
tin-foil to the plate. She offered her one of them, saying:
"Pripremicémo ih mi od samljevenog mesanog mesa.
Hm! Hm! Tako su dobre, sa svim mirisima sume koji
imaju."

"Imaju sve miris sume," Katharina commented.

"Govorite dobro nas jezik," the woman said.

"Stvarno? Nisam to primetila," answered Katharina,
uncertain, and she sighed: "Steta sto ovde pored postoje
ta ogromna vrata za koja neznas kud te mogu odvesti."
Then she asked: "Ko li uopste moze ziveti tamo?"

"Nisam nikad bila unutra," the woman was defensive, "od skora sam ovde. Mislim da taj tako neprijatan miris koji dolazi iza tih velikih vrata je od boje koja se nanosi na tek ustavljenu kozu, ali ja na srecu nemam prozore. Vidite, iza one zuckaste flase bila je spijunka, ali ja sam i nju zatvorila."[1]

She left the wine-shop at the corner of the little square that was trying to be a garden. The grass was sparse, growing in tufts. A few flowers surrounded the central statue. A notice warned 'the plants are poisonous' . . .

"I'm going away," Katharina thought, "perhaps there's poison in the soil too, that's why the grass won't grow. There's something in the air here, that restricts it. You have to close the doors before dusk and open them at dawn."

The library was still open. She went up the stone staircase. She felt a familiar touch under the soles of her feet as far as the entrance.

"We're closed for lending books," they told her. "If you just want to consult the catalogue . . ."

"I'd like to speak to the chief librarian," she said and sat down to wait.

"We're closing," they told her a few minutes later. "It's no use your waiting any longer today. Come back tomorrow."

---

[1] "We make them ourselves with a mixture of meats minced specially. They are good."/"They have all the smells of the woods."/"You speak our language well."/"Really? I hadn't realized."/"A pity that there is that corridor next door . . ."/"Who ever can live in there?"/"I've never been in there . . . I've only been here a short while. I think it is that coloured varnish that they add after the tanning of the skins. The smell is disgusting and I have no windows. You see, behind that yellow bottle there was a spy-hole, but I've closed it."

'Tomorrow', she was surprised to hear that short word. She went out, absentminded, passing a group of school-children.

A little further along, the building. She wrote her name in the white register and went up the stairs. Her gloved hand slid along the silken red bannister. She took off her glove to enjoy the pleasant feeling. At that time of day there was no-one in the building. A dripping of water. Almost as if it were a museum open just for her. She went slowly up the spiral staircase of pale marble.

There was only one attendant, he kept an eye on things from the ground floor. He had no intention of going upstairs; the visitor had made a favourable impression on him. "Better that way," she thought, "I've always hated looking at pictures with someone behind me. They measure the time, how long you stand still. And if the minutes go by, they start worrying as if you were devouring their precious works of art. They get on your nerves."

The stairs were in darkness, the curtains drawn, impossible to shift them; every curtain had an iron weight in the hem. "One way to ensure that you drown." The lack of light obscured the pictures, the dark and the damp stripped memory away. It was too dark to see the portraits.

"A dead collection. It's useless for me to stay here," she decided. 'They see to it that visitors have their eyes shrouded with a net."

She searched in vain for a portrait of Maximilian. "It's down in the storerooms," the attendant told her. "The director does allow people to go down into the storeroom, but at the moment he is in Budapest for a concert."

She went back along the walls of one of the rooms. She knew the places where the doors were, she knew what she would find if she opened one. She tried it and she was right. The drawn line led into the distance. She would find other distinct lines, but not going beyond the enclosed area. She knew the only opening which was not a way out.

In the large hall the windowsills were wide. You could slip between the pillars and see the room of mirrors, red and gold velvets reflected in the diamond-cut facets of the Bohemian glass.

Katharina was outside and her body breathed, but her eyes were red and the glass hurt her pale pupils.

9

The big gate closed behind her. Now she could enter the building. She breathed a different air. She had the freedom to discover cupboards full of precious materials and other things strange to her sense of smell.

She had to do everything quickly. She walked down the long corridor to the window. She rested against the windowsill and was hit, like a shock, by the air with its smells from the garden. She leaned out over the drop. Beyond the twisted branches that prevented access to anybody who dared try to get in, was the sea. But she did not manage to see it that day either; her sight still found no freedom.

She resumed her walk past the tapestries silent in their ancient meditations. The wall coverings were drapes tied together in plaits and between them came the rustling of the wind. The air injected, stealthily, some faint life into objects which sighed to one another. Full of foreboding in their long showcases, cold Bohemian glass waited.

"These old rooms do not find peace," she thought, "they should concentrate in well-earned silence, they should understand that their efforts cannot succeed against a forgotten history." It was impossible to break up this silence, except perhaps with the flight of the seagulls, outside.

These ferments were strange to her, she could not resolve their paroxysms with useless injections. The icy silence of the glass showcases was not unlike the watery reflections in the park.

"I shall manage to see the sea again," she told herself, "and shall find the suitcase that I left in this building, just behind the door in the big room." In that corner room, from the bed one could make out the sea.

She moved aside the plaits that hung like drapery making the room dark, and entered a large square space. After the darkness of the hall, that space seemed to her immense, but it was not.

She found herself in a big room. "Had I not just come in," she thought, "I would have said that there were neither doors nor windows."

She felt herself pushed backwards, the soft walls received her with an old silence. She had her damp overcoat over her shoulders and, as she turned around, it fell, covering a showcase.

The sheets of glass, angled and with bevelled borders, were guarding sets of coins encased in velvet.

She hid her modest overcoat behind the curtain. The lesson in self-assurance, which she had given herself, was lost like her in the darkness of that collection. The glass had misted up with the dampness of her overcoat. She hastened to clean it, but her warm hand only produced large, opaque circles.

Through the slightly uneven glass she could just make out the various metals. She started to follow the sequence of the collection, holding her fingers against the plate glass in order to get rid of the reflections. The labels with names half-erased indicated the chronology, demonstrated the routes of commerce and the mingling of dynasties and families.

The oldest coins showed profiles of nymphs with objects from the sea woven into their hair, or dolphins. Empty Gorgon mouths marked the centre of the silver. The gods of the oracles acquired the same look as generals.

"The fate of currency," she thought, "is at one with that of laws and standards." Heads crowned with laurel or surmounted by head-dresses ruled over chanceries, moved troops. Madness, too, was drawn in the blonde patina of copper and malachite: meteors worshipped, animals massacred in the circus. The sharp image on a coin with worn edges surprised her; on the back the female genitals flowered on a drape.

She had difficulty in following it all, the glass was becoming opaque. She could see the centres of the coins becoming less clear under the tired presses, the alloys turning base, the names becoming confused through violence.

Under the pretence of orthodoxy, series of faces were produced, absorbed in the significance of their role, with globes and crosses. The metal was thin, the large letters came together in a circular decoration. The portraits of the bishops Giobardo, Volrico, Leonardo, Arlongo carried the reliefs of their coat-of-arms; the same fear of emptiness. On the reverse was the hill, and the city raising flags on its walls and opening three gates.

The rustling in the plaited fabric increased. And the wind expanded the sheets of metal like the routes of commerce, it curled wigs and brocades and bellied the sails of the galleons. The marriage between Venice and the sea was scarcely perceptible.

Beyond the curtains that jealously preserved the shade, she could hear rain falling, going straight down into the gutter and gushing over the grating. She remembered the puddle, that part of the house had always needed attention.

On different velvet a small light illuminated the aspirations of the Habsburgs. To have eyes without shadows, that is what the empress Maria Theresia would have loved, and the engraver had cut her profile like a diadem. The great thaler from 1780 also had letters engraved on its edges. "It's what you wanted," she murmured, "not just the kingdoms of Bohemia, Hungary, the Tyrol, the heart of Europe, but also the dreamed of countries overseas." Her grandfather had shown her a silver coin from Africa, the same as this one, even if the effigy was that of an Italian king. "They have imitated the thaler of Maria Theresia," he had explained to her, "because for the natives this was the only coin." Franz Ioseph had distant eyes and the coinage rendered them even colder.

She lost herself in those profiles, in those coats-of-arms, nightmares that surfaced from the sea and left their sign imprinted on the rocks, above the play of waves and emotions. The inscriptions and glances filled the void with power, almost suggesting to her the name that she could not find at the meeting of languages and roads. The dynasties interrelated in the same way as the facts that she linked together, then faded away. And so those series finished and started again with each different minting. "Fresh from the mint, they really seem to be mirrors," her grandfather had told her. "Do the collectors value them for that?" "No, not only for that." In those mirrors one sought the name, and lost the image.

The rain was beating unevenly against the windows and her thoughts were struggling against a surface of absence.

The collection continued higher up. Boxes were hung over the showcases where the wall was more protected from the light. The wood was dark and the well-fitted glass stopped the air from circulating. Here it was not coins that were lined up, but butterflies. Black pins pushed through those shadowy features. Every row repeated similar examples, only the attention of an entomologist could distinguish the varieties. Variations of colour and intensity in the veining created a series. "Each one," she thought, "adapts itself to the light of its surroundings and experiments in harmony with nature. They exist in the colour for instant after instant. Perhaps it is because of this that they say that butterflies burn . . ." "You will burn like a butterfly," she was told when she was a child.

The butterflies in the glass cases she had once chased in fields, or she had seen them closed at dawn, like wrapped thoughts. The thoughts of the dead, that is what the peasant women called them. Now the little cards with their classification and date of capture made her uncomfortable, the names more piercing than the pins.

Filigrees covered in powdery white constituted the elegance of the genus *Parnassius*, with black and pink eyes in the *Apollo* and a pale transparency in the little *Mnemosyne*. The yellow *Papilii* were edged with black lace, the *Machaon* deeply coloured, slender the *Podalirius*. The *Pieridae* and the *Rodoceres* had wings folded like leaves and the half-mourning of the *Galateas* blended with the speckled tufts of the background. Amongst the stones and the grass rested the burnt tonalities of the *Danaïs* and the *Aglais*. The *Vanessae* and the *Apaturae* displayed velvet and mother-of-pearl, and their attractiveness related them to the butterflies that flew high in the tropical forests. Embroideries and

tails allowed one to recognize other Papilionidae whose
colours had captured a light that still brightened the glass
cupboards.

All along this procession, more than by any other
ornament, Katharina was surprised by the eyes imprinted
on the wings. These shadowy glances were even more
penetrating on the moths; they were large and strong and
displayed their colour when flying. The *Deilephilae* and
the *Sphingidae* absorbed the pink of the evening. The
Acherontiae atropos declared herself the princess of darkness. In the moonlight the *Catocalae* gleamed with cold
hues and the Saturnidae, the night peacocks, opened their
eyes wide and spread the great span of their wings.

The wall was embroidered with those eyes; or, rather,
those interwining glances constituted the wall.

The mirror coins and the mirror wings glistened in
different ways and reflected their cries on Katharina. She
drew back into the wallhangings and crossed the corridor
again. Beyond the windows, the branches were shiny and
black with rain.

She had herself announced again. An undefinable figure
accompanied her to a nearly dark hall.

She stood waiting. There were no chairs pushed
against the wallhangings. She waited for a long time,
until, preceded by a servant, he arrived.

Katharina backed away along the soft surface that
opened up in the darkness. They were facing each other.
They hesitated before speaking, neither of them had
decided which language to use. Perhaps they realized they
had nothing to say to each other and perhaps looked each
other straight in the eyes for the first time.

The pallor of his face disguised its features. The wrinkles went from his nose towards his mouth, marking a grimace of disgust. The round thick spectacles hid those eyes that she could not remember ever having seen except behind strong glass.

He spoke first. Katharina noticed that his voice trembled a little; she was pleased and said:

"Ich freue mich, dich bei guter Gesundheit zu sehen."[1]

The folds in his face responded, showing a hint of dismay. The servant who stood by him made as if to take a step closer towards him.

Then Katharina moved. She sensed another person in the room. She felt the presence, but did not have the time to see the figure properly before it flattened itself into the darkness. She could not even guess the sex, perhaps it was a boy.

His face contracted and the folds stretched to fine lines. The lips, already tight as a warning, closed in a dry wound. Something was not going the way he wanted.

Because of a small mistake, Katharina had the better of both him and the unseen, waiting figure. She was relieved a little.

He, meanwhile, was trying to gain time. He leant his walking-stick with its shiny handle against the glass of a showcase, but it slid to the floor noiselessly.

They both avoided mentioning the name of the child, conscious that naming him in that air filled with bitterness would have sounded out of tune, plaintive like a violin chord. Locked behind masks of spite, and with silence as their last sophisticated weapon,

---

[1] I'm pleased to see you in good health.

they fought without conviction each to have the upper hand.

He kept on murmuring things like: "Ich kann nicht mehr tun . . . Ich ertrage deinen Anblick nicht."[1] They were words, some neither clear nor articulated with precision, that reminded her of the uneven edges of the coins. What he was thinking of saying was moving away from things and images, sliding further away from the rigour of the conversation that those collections expressed. The unravelling of the words identified his sickness.

When Katharina saw him lean his back against the chair to sit with more authority, she had the distinct feeling that their discussion was not taking any shape, that it remained suspended in disconnected words and that it was already following only loosely defined directions. Now she wanted to go, to return to her very own reason for coming here, which these words were disturbing like dust. She tried to say something which would not only bring back the past, but which would work on neutral ground. The words did not come, they were drops of salt swallowed by an injured throat.

She searched her memory for that name, erased on the official documents. Her nose might start bleeding again. She was groping in the labyrinth that he him- self wanted to conceal with the logic of the stronger person. She put together the mosaic of early cries; some had been lost. The injuries they had inflicted on her were covered by the ether of time, but an open wound remained where one could see the living flesh pulsate, a fragile space which, day after day, thin needles widened.

---

[1] I can do no more . . . I cannot stand your look.

Because of that small tessera missing from the mosaic of cruelties, Katharina, like somebody who has been waiting a long time to learn something new, pronounced the name first, and said in a clear, icy tone:

"Der Junge weiss nichts. Davon darf er nichts erfahren. Und ich werde dir nie erlauben, auch ihn, sein Leben zu zerstören."[1]

She could no longer hold back the words which were rolling out. She gasped for air, her hands holding the edge of the table. She felt the heat from the lamp and moved away. The light deepened a line on his face, something her poor newly found words could not grasp or disclose.

A gesture seemed for a moment to be attracting the attention of the other servant, at least she assumed that that was what he was. He had left in silence, but she suspected his presence where, hidden by the man's shoulders, she could not see him.

The walking-stick had slipped onto the floor. Katharina did nothing to pick it up, she wanted to witness his difficulty in moving. If he had asked her to help him, she might, perhaps, have broken that stiffness, inflated and tense like an abcess. She might not have noticed how badly he needed the walking-stick. But the nervous fluttering of his fingers betrayed him. She started. A knot that had been tightened for years seemed loosened.

They remained opposite each other. Behind them, other rare collections surfaced from the dark, so rare as to appear incomprehensible.

'Ja, deine Welt ist schon interessant. Alles ist im

---

[1] The boy knows nothing. He is not allowed to know anything. And I would never let you ruin his life as well.

Verzeichnis festgehalten, jedes Exemplar lebt nicht, sondern kennt nur seinen Platz,"[1] she said in an attempt to introduce the thrust of her voice into the silence.

He did not answer, his hands running along the shiny wood. Walking sideways, he found support from the cold glass cases. He went as far as the dark piece of furniture at the end of the room, and let himself down onto a stiff high chair. A short time had passed, and yet now his face had acquired the hardness of the effigies engraved on the coins.

On the large table was a cheque-book, a little dagger was holding its thin pages in place. She noticed that the chequebook was untouched, and directed her glance carefully to his hands which, while waiting, were absent-mindedly fingering a small gun. It was perhaps a woman's weapon but could have been a military one, for an officer in full uniform.

In an attempt to deflect her eyes that were fixed on him, he started to talk of the complicated factors surrounding the need for those collections. He talked about them as a weight that could not become detached from its origin. In those glass cupboards there was one idea only, a name, its uninterrupted echo. He was speaking Serbian, he was speaking his language. "One more trap," Katharina thought, but would have liked to answer with the certainty that that name, from wanting to last too long, had squashed itself against the velvet and fallen asleep for ever in the pungent smell of camphor.

"Ich habe wenig Zeig," he added, "und das ist mein

---

[1] Yes, your world is interesting. Everything is catalogued, no specimen lives, but each knows its place.

letztes Zugestädnis."[1] He put down the pistol in order to pick up the cheque-book with its thin pages.

"Ich komme zu den Tatsachen,"[2] Katharina concluded harshly. "Ich will, dass diese Dokumente unterschrieben werden. Ich will nach jahrelangem Warten mein Kind wiedersehen."[3]

He tried to press the bell amongst those bizarre plaits of silk that terrorized her like arabesques from a frozen forest.

Katharina took hold of the gun and stopped him. Slowly she withdrew, keeping him covered with the weapon. For the last time she stared at that face which had given her so much pain. She looked at his shaking hands, the right one was thin and of a darker colour.

She slid her body along the walls. She was back in the dark hall.

The undefined figure, it could have been a servant, held out her modest overcoat still wet with rain.

A film of yellowish dust had settled on the swollen tapestries, the weariness of sick generations. Along the corridor the old furniture was looking at her, saddened by loneliness, and she felt responsible. They seemed to be saying to her "We know well the flights, and the sorrowful returns . . . Careful, Katharina . . . the green grasslands are far away now. We shared the action with you . . . you touched us . . . you always came close and we welcomed you."

Katharina pressed her fists against her ears, just as she used to as a child, and hurried past the door with the

---

[1] I have little time, . . . and this is my last concession.

[2] I'm coming to the point.

[3] I want these documents signed. After so many years of waiting, I want to see my child again.

concave windows, where the sun less and less frequently reflected the dust into a myriad of colours like a rainbow. She heard the click of the door shutting behind her. She knew how those high beds would wait patiently, puffed out with frozen linen; they had welcomed her delicate, pregnant body. How orphanlike those objects looked, neglected and left to themselves! The wind ruled over them and they winked and conspired, determined to get their revenge.

The difficult part was over. Now she had to go out into the open.

She cleared the last steps without turning around. Somebody had taught her that one must never look back.

Now she felt safe. Through those large slits, the windows of the house, nobody could reach her any more.

10

A crowded street received her. The loud shouting deaf-
ened her, colours confused her. She sat on a low wall.
From behind her somebody took away the suitcase she
had found with such difficulty. Everybody saw it, and
their silence was a conspiracy.

The tram arrived; it made a great deal of noise just as
it used to in the past.

Katharina got on with nothing in her hands, she put
them into the pockets of her wet overcoat with the
jewel-like buttons.

She looked at the windows of the houses and at the
balconies, on which the emperor's smile seemed to rest.
But the wrinkles, so ironed out, were only able to show
an indifferent approval. It was just like the imprisoned
smile in the room with the showcases she had left behind.

In the folds of those wrinkles had settled the fears
that bring ghosts to life. In its difficult evolution the
world was reaching a happy limit, the life of commerce
was invigorating a bloodless reality, and at that very
moment he imposed his own impassive figure, cloaked in
turquoise, lofty on his white horse. And when a hand
was raised against his impeccable uniform, remorseful, he
had a votive church built, the Votivkirche. He en-
compassed the world with his glance and hardly bowed,
a slight nod to the facts and ideas which were stirring
the nations.

He classified forms and turned their troublesome growth into an inane order. Chanceries, offices and courts became accustomed to breathing that air that he benignly donated. The deeds intended for progress withered with boredom.

With him the men behind the desks and those who lived for commerce felt threatened when excited by the pale beer served by obsequious youths in leather aprons; something could menace their well-being, a sudden shadow might fall.

And when that desire to live, to attain the dream overseas, found a new impetus in which every jolt of the great Empire placed its trust, there was nothing one could do but stoop to a dark destiny, to the freezing protocols. Fathers of families breathed deeply, and a slight anaesthetic guaranteed that nothing could injure them any longer.

With glassy eyes within a triangle of wrinkles, he kept scanning the orbit of a static mechanism, slowing it down, breaking the dark force of power into rivulets that, without recognizing each other, ran parallel. The deviations and the differences mattered no longer, were to be seen behind the grids that science and its institutions secured. The spirit of adventure remained in a vacuum, preserved forever.

'Danke schön, es ist alles sehr schön gewesen."[1]

A God-fearing, placid and lawful enjoyment came back. A kind of ether had been sprayed on the world and on the city, its sorrowful core.

---

[1] "Thank you very much, it's all been very nice."

The waltz concealed the fears. What was dying slowly in the daily monotony found life again thanks to the Imperial Royal People's Lottery. Books of dreams were invented, a concession to the Bohemian gypsies and an invitation to the men of science not to forget the double nature of soul and history.

The months of the calendars displayed delicate colours, capable of inspiring fantasies like the reflections of goblets in the shop windows recalling anniversaries and time spent at the spas. The docile bodies, dressed in the same blue as the immobile figure from which they took silent leave, set out along the streets; moving from the centre to the peripheries, following the branches of a minutely subdivided network. These clockwork figures, wound up for a fixed time, brought letters sealed with that red which no longer evoked any emotion, but had the sole function of enclosing barren regulations. The messengers' faces all had the same paralysed smile, and on their neverending journey their feet became swollen with air like those of the dead. At the end of their mission, the message they carried was perhaps already redundant because of the instructions that new submissive bodies were ready to deliver. Tranquillity was secured by those written documents which silently shrivelled up. He forbade the colour red but in the Mexican arenas red magnified the roaring of the crowd. This colour came through everywhere. In November, nature kept declaring it with the same insistence shown by the earth among the stones in the Karst. Dynasties, too, become anaemic and at the slightest push they let a pale liquid escape from their veins, as a result of not taking nourishment from this energy. Their lives grow through injustice and denial. But, as with every good middle-class person who would measure himself against a different brother, a shadow appears in the dialogue. At times our imagination is so cloudy that it leaves us in a light sleep, where anybody can enter, like the light of dawn through the slats of shutters. And it is necessary to expel the colourless matter, it kills the wish and with it the will.

The gypsies, their bags filled with multi-coloured ribbons, declare that the sweet prince whose eyes are too pale still lives, and in the harbour, amongst the unused, rusty drums, their whispers tell the truth; they hear the unhappy princess Charlotte's cries of madness from the balcony of the castle by the sea.[1]

The gypsy women approach quickly, their jewelled hands keep turning those spheres in which the inverted world is reflected. Their eyes are mirrored in the glass balls they offer. They keep moving amongst the tables out in the open. And at night they go far away, leaving wishes behind among the mirrors of the cafés.

The book of dreams that he invented begins to appear on the scene at the time when the windows in the cafés mist over, covered by a haze of moods and smells, and one hears the sound of violins calling far away in the distance.

Then, as if for a quadrille, faces arrive that are still adolescent and looking for death. Their conviction reinforced desire, and inspired nausea for the false satisfactions of progress. Hatred grew with the speed of an abcess. They turned towards Greece, a truth to be recomposed, but to no avail. "Leicht vergisst der Mensch, dass er am Leben war, die Welt, dass er gelebt,"[2] was

---

[1] The castle referred to here is that of Miramare by the architect Karl Junker, built in 1856 for the archduke Maximilian of Habsburg. (Tr.)

[2] "Man easily forgets that he lived, and the world he lived in."

the faint annotation in one of those notebooks.

It is said that he loved in Maximilian the image of youth that he had lost in himself. In the palace rooms where people plotted, some saw his glassy eyes shine for the space of a night and harden again. The adventure on the Pacific had been decided upon. And a coloured wheel of fire riddled that head which had given up everything but hope.

The gypsies keep wearing their colourful bright skirts with the long-forbidden red, and swirl them out in circles, like spinning tops that used to make us dream as children. It is a whirl that provides meaning, now that the market where one walks is a modern kasbah. Crimes are not plotted behind curtains thick with history. In the noisy city streets, on every corner, we are under the watchful eye of a Swiss clock which the still-helpless Slav buys, thinking it must be good.

The traffic of languages went hand in hand with the trade of goods. The 's'ciavi', that is what they were called, anticipated the needs. Katharina was surprised by the quantity of clocks hanging on display. With new strength, Serbs, Croats, Slavs once again claimed their commercial relationship to the city that had kept them away in an uncaring, distracted manner.

She had not entered the quarter kept separate from the rest of the city. Only the houses in the old centre, with their cracked walls, their swollen planks, attracted her attention. She walked on the broken pavements, climbed the steps, deciphered faded numbers, looked at the sad shapes of evergreens in vases behind windows. That map, exact in all its size and detail, offered reassurance: that of a memory easily reconstructed in a drawing. The other area, though, could not guarantee landmarks; it was like those uncharted areas in old topographical works covered by hurried outlines.

The maps that she remembered all suggested this indecision. Zones, clearly mapped with outlines and demarcations, were joined to spaces where no rules were discernible, a contrast which seemed to imply the need for an organism. And this city drawn in a single act of thinking, managed to make discomfort feel more than ever natural.

In that quarter, the very lack of defined borders (and of the natural selection that the concentration of people and things requires) made trade flourish. The currents of industry and commerce joined in a vast river-bed. Every activity, even the illicit traffic that had circulated in narrow and dark alleys, was expanding beyond its boundaries. It was the gusts of fashion, the needs of consumers that spread in a swarm of market stalls.

The seeds that the American wave had scattered from a small core, fertilized a pervasive yet colourless mass like a layer of silt. In that wave everything seemed homogenized, with no distinctions allowed and every relationship avoided.

The houses had been built on the cheap, and low, in order to avoid maintenance costs. Doors and windows opened at random on their façades, which cracked immediately. The plaster crumbled and the wind made fragments waver and fall away. Buildings in ruin, half-demolished, with once lived-in rooms imprinted on their sides, had seen bits added on that only imitated the pretence of the city. Tiled balconies, coloured gratings and windows enlarged out of all proportion deformed the pale wrinkled skin of the façades.

Small shops followed one another. In the slightly protruding shop windows the most varied merchandise mingled smells and colours. In the groceries the perfumed spices scarcely concealed fluid smells. In the dressmakers' shops, of which there were plenty, coloured and shiny cloths unrolled until they formed unnatural creases in order to show the quality of the fabric. In the great majority of the shops objects of various origins and styles were juxtaposed in unpredictable ways, having in common only the concern to hide their use through the abundance and strangeness of their decoration. Frames and stuccoes of reddish gilding jostled with tortoiseshell and boxes of mother-of-pearl. Statues of ivory leant against leather bindings of a similar colour. Dinner services, made up of different pieces, looked good against silver trays. Animal skins hung over these contrasting objects.

Everyone seemed to have arrived by chance at that crossroads of interests, of languages and of logic, even those who had been established for generations and who had learnt to read the hidden laws of this market place. And everybody chose and bought according to their intentions of the moment. They appreciated those objects that seemed to be more than they were in reality, with the curiosity of someone landing from another world.

Some, called 'strangers', who were not foreigners but had simply a different social standing, disguised themselves while wandering around looking for some ornament that, even if alien to their customs, could fulfil a desire. Their hesitations, though, made them recognizable and—not without an ironic wink—the prices were doubled for them.

In that neighbourhood there were still trams. A victory for the local councillors, or just another testimony to their conservatism, even if the trams did not look as they used to. The carriages looked as if they were made of cardboard for some public performance and, when they clanked through the city, the people sitting inside took on the stiff air of travellers from afar.

The café was crowded at that time of the day. Women were returning with baskets of long vegetables smelling of the market, mixed up with spices to use in goulash. The wine drowned all the smells.

Katharina drank her first glass of chilled wine for the day. "I'll come back later," she thought, "when the women with the shopping have gone home."

She had the impression of being in front of a faded scene, lifeless and fixed by a photograph, one of those ancestral photographs where the settled dust gives beauty even to faces that never were beautiful. She became aware that she was lingering to watch certain images, and that she was seeing them undergo a doubling; as if there were many layers of invisible film that tricked her vision if she moved slightly in relation to the fixed point of the image.

She would have liked to go in to buy some spices. "But what could I do with them?" she asked herself. On the doors of certain small rooms used as dressmakers' and shoemakers' premises, shop assistants were winking expertly.

She went into one at random. It was a dressmaker's shop. The shop assistant smiled at her and, without asking what she wanted, he spread out in front of her a smooth and shiny material, in a vulgar colour.

She was amused with the thought of wearing a dress like that and chose it. The man took her measurements, sliding his hands with over-long fingers down her hips; he paused on the waist absentmindedly tying the tape-measure. "How did you manage not to entangle it?" she let out. "Perhaps he is a magician disguised as a shop assistant?" His breath smelt bitter.

The tape-measure unwound itself, fell on the coloured materials. With the practised instinct of the job, he stretched out his hands to a blue roll and wrapped it around Katharina. "He knows his job well. Next he'll tell me that I have blue eyes," she thought, "and that their colour will stand out more." She had always hated to dress in blue, like in fairy tales.

"This material is too slippery," she heard him whisper. "I have something finer for you. I always keep something more select in my shop for customers like yourself." And he pointed enticingly to the inside of the shop.

Katharina entered. The next room was large, the ceiling high. She would never have thought that a back room could extend in such a concertina-like fashion. A big room full of high shelves right up to the ceiling.

She put her head right back to be able to look up: "If only there had been a window to light up the store," she thought, but did not see one. Massive boxes touched the dusty ceiling; seeing them from below they looked like old forgotten archives, files of a totally different kind.

She wanted to climb up onto the metal shelving structure like a squirrel in search of the unusual, the forbidden. She suddenly turned towards the shop assistant, she almost took him by surprise. She felt herself going red. She would rather have been in the café drinking wine, mixing with the people from the bustling neighbourhood in the late morning.

The shop assistant was close to her. She felt again his strong breath. The cloth that he had been embracing shortly before had now fallen next to some oriental rubbish, strange cushions, rejects, and had formed a large welcoming platform, like a duvet into which one could sink.

"Do you want something unusual?" The voice of the shop assistant made her jolt. "I believe there are very interesting magazines up there, the boss was a collector. Something exciting?" He had clearly given up the idea of making the dress. The red had mixed itself with the blue, the materials were lying on the floor, the stream of the cloth had freed itself from his hands and had unrolled and formed almost a train around Katharina's feet.

She could have been a statue or an antique figure about to have her portrait painted. Her empty eyes had the fixedness of a painting.

Meanwhile the shop assistant had sat down on one of the sofas, and his face was increasingly taking on feminine features. An ambiguous attraction drew her towards this individual with the low forehead and a nose touching a non-existent mouth, from which the teeth seemed to have disappeared. When he talked one had the impression of a gash. His hair was thick, almost glued to the temples, he still oiled it. Everything that Katharina rejected in a man was in front of her, and she sat down on that sofa stained with powder and aromatic oils.

On the other side of the large concertina-like room, one could see a miserable work-room. Nobody was sewing and the sewing-machine was used just to lean on.

The red velvet on the sofa was torn in several places. Loose horsehair burst out as if wanting to be pulled by some insolent hand.

She kept looking at the large ceiling beams. Not much time had passed since the days when their strength had been tested by loads of maize. The voyages of the ships had been all too frequent.

"From maize to silk," she thought, "basically a dazzling step backwards." And she pressed her right forefinger into the deep hole of the sofa, turned it mechanically like a screw and felt the bottom of that dark cavity. Suddenly she was thirsty, her throat dried out; she felt desire dimming her sight.

The rolls of silks threw themselves over her; slimy, sweet bodies from whose poisonous smoothness it was difficult to free oneself. Gaudy and shiny, they touched her legs like uncontrollable eels, they slid along the floor unravelling. Their touch gave her a feeling of over-whelming tension. They caressed her skin, which became passive. Then the starch and the rigid pleats gave life to an inner energy, a muscular tension that left her feeling exhausted.

The folds in the cloth made the mannequins appear to be filled with this rediscovered vitality: skin, child, breast-feeding it, carrying it.

The violent colours made her sight hazy. Coloured balloons went up and only stopped at the sight of the worm-eaten beams, fearful that they had dared go so far up.

The air in the workshop was stale. From the street, like gusts of sand, the smell of herbs came in, sharp to the point of nausea.

From the main beam hung immensely long cobwebs. It was unthinkable that spiders, one at a time, could have woven that net. Someone had climbed up there deliberately. Or it might be only an old print of a ship turned upside down.

She looked anxiously for her glasses. She remembered that the lenses had been broken when the leather bag had spilled. The boy could even have trampled on them when he had helped her gather the scattered things.

She thought again about the Serbian doctor who had examined her eyes. She heard clearly his soft voice: "Katha . . . tvoe oci su svetle, previse svetle . . . your look is too uncovered . . ."[1]

She felt the brown body press against hers, even now she noticed the impact, like cold water on a hot face.

In front of her the green of the Slovenian fields opened up and, in the distant blue, she saw again small busy men walking across the countryside in the direction of a hill. The house where they were going was barely visible. It was a long way and they lost sight of their destination more than once. They found a path amongst the rustling leaves. Dusk was approaching and they stopped in front of the house, but at the same time they disappeared, as if they had been drawn by a pen on a damp window and the first snow had covered them.

"There, I've arrived, the freshness of the hill, the house, they have waited for me for too long. There will be cobwebs." And she smiled at the pleasure of sweeping them away by climbing up into the most unlikely corners.

She entered confidently, and immediately tripped over the overturned door. She hurt herself on the rusty lock; a long scratch on her right hand started to bleed. A dead bird was lying against the window frame. On the

---

[1] "Katha . . . your eyes are pale, too pale . . ."

sideboard, which was missing a leg, there was a jug, full to the brim with a liquid the colour of November plums.

She went inside without colliding with anything. She sat down at the bottom of the stairs leading up to the bedrooms. She took off her shoes, heavy and soaked from the dampness of the long grass, and held her tired feet in her hands as she had as a child.

Dusk had fallen and the house had no more light. She heard a sharp call; her name like a breath came from the top of the stairs, where thick darkness lay. She took a few steps. The wood had been broken recently, the day before or maybe only a few hours ago, the crack was white and porous and the wood still gave out its scent.

With her shoes in her left hand, leaving the right one free to open doors, she went up to the far end, from where she could hear the voice. The door was open. She put her hands inside each shoe, like boxing gloves they would protect her.

Someone asked her something again, sharply.

She ran away. She ran across the damp green of the fields. Now the leaves, wet with rain, no longer caressed her, they pricked her soaking skin like invisible pins. Along the slope the bushes were blocking her way, they seemed to grow as you looked at them. She reached the stream running over large snow-white stones, and washed her face with the cold, pure water. From the round stones the light-coloured eyes kept on looking at her.

The noise from the street came clear, suddenly. Girls came and went. They were shop assistants with gaudy make-up. They announced their presence in an aggressive way and had dark beauty-spots on their thick skin.

A woman went by dressed in sequins and pink-coloured 'ciaffe'.[1] She was wearing a hat with a veil. Her hesitant walk seemed to ask forgiveness for appearing at that time of the day. She was alone. The prostitutes loved her and it was said that sometimes they lent her a client. And yet, behind the dark veil, one flutter of her eyelids could destroy the self-assurance of the youngest among them.

---

[1] The word in the local dialect for cheap, gaudy jewellery.

11

Outside the wind had loosened its grip. It was well into day.

She tried to get a taxi, without success. "Every city the same problem, one country is like the next, one city is no better than another. It would be good to think that one could cross the streets of the world on one's own legs, with the safety of one's own body. The old knights left their past and travelled through space like an invention. They were not only concerned with moving about, they were eager to learn. Then they used horses and that was different; the horse would live their life and they the horse's, and the journey would become love, sharing."

"I must walk . . . and if I meet Bertrand Smoleck I will not recognize him, I would not be able to fit together his features. His figure has already dissolved like dust in the sun."

One thing she wanted to know: whether he had forgotten his overcoat. It could happen even to a maestro born in Berlin. Were the Berliners not serious people? He himself had been eager to confirm that. "Maestri from Berlin," he had said, "compose music, not words." Consequently he had no reason to abandon an overcoat on the handle of any door; but then that overcoat was so much a part of him.

"Anyhow, I am not going on the same route, I will not meet him."

"The old shadows have come back while closing my eyes for just a moment on the low sofa."

"I don't care if I don't know anyone, what good would it do, I have a few hours left, I must speak to the lawyer . . . And then . . . when one is called to a town . . . one does not retain the details . . . the conviction with which one walks, the pauses . . . Other people are aware. I am here and I am waiting for something which concerns me and should not concern the law. I could say that to anyone.

"A mirror . . . Was there one in the dresssmaker's shop? I don't think so. I didn't see it. I had it in my bag, I seem to remember, but it dropped in the crack where my heel was caught.

"There was once a Slav princess, as slim as a mulberry tree. She had large and beautiful eyes, and people looked at themselves in those two green pools. A prince rode past and did not recognize himself. His uniform did not stand out. Those still lakes did not please the Nordic prince and he ran them through. Since then he has wandered around in the night and the white horse has had no rest; he follows those huge eyes of the Slav princess."

She remained seated at the small, green marble table. Beyond the avenue, as soon as the train moved, she would be able to glimpse the sea again. The railway carriages on the tracks suffered unending stops, waiting for the man in a grey uniform to take them away to the sleepy station.

She no longer remembered the exact time of the appointment. She glanced at her neighbour's newspaper. The tall and slouching figure opened the pages and the headlines stood out in the light: TROOPS GATHERING ON THE FRONTIERS. A fold in the newspaper stopped her from reading on and finding which frontiers. Immediately below, in round, large letters MAD RUN ON THE CURRENCY.

She sat down and her thoughts raced and sank precipitately. "Just like money." She realized that she was looking for a name, his; she called it but it became confused with the child's . . . Friedrich . . .

On account of Friedrich she found herself in a town that did not recognize her, where this waiting bewildered her. In the café with its misty walls the smoke never wanted to leave. Someone opened the windows but the veil of smoke did not disappear, it remained in the air, crouched down, rose up, thickened, and took refuge behind the chipped plaster, waiting for the windows to close before coming back quickly amongst the tables to give the marble its old humidity. Her eyes became irritated at once and they were surrounded by a red halo, as if she had been crying. It felt good to stay in the café and wait in the void, to look at the hanging *Zeitungsspanner* with the news of the day already gone.

Her face took on different features, but it was because of the peculiar mirror. She moved the wicker chair a little. A poster on the wall captured her attention, its design depended on areas of pure colour. She was determined not to look at that glass stained with magic. "When I was a child I had a cat . . . for fun I would put it in front of a mirror and, suspicious, it would check behind it with its paw . . . I shall do the same."

Behind the large window crowds of people were going by. A fine rain made people hurry. The provident opened their umbrellas, hiding themselves under them and looking with childish superiority at the incautious one who walked leaning sideways, trying to shelter under non-existent eaves.

It was the brightly coloured woman who had recommended her that café. "That way," she had said, "you will be able to observe."

The plaster was hanging like fringes. The humidity penetrated in a lady-like fashion, with the draughts, its smell entered her nostrils. Her childhood allergy increased.

Her newspaper stick struck the figure in black behind her. He was a man of less than average height. The years had left their mark on his face, over his colourless complexion. Perhaps there were eyes behind those two dark glasses.

A hand gloved with grey wool was clutching a walking-stick with an ancient handle. His movements were steady, he alternated between holding the stick and the tea cup. He drank in small sips, swallowing in the manner of the Chinese, almost as if he had hiccups. His body occupied the entire wicker chair, he had sunk into it as if born in that position. He tapped on the marble tabletop. She was surprised at the waiter's speed. He handed him the newspaper, its pages had been ironed, the headlines unusually large, the typesetter had inflated the news.

The allergy and the irritation on her hands came back. Her eyes were watering.

The large body was showing through the slots in the back of the chair, slices of darkly dressed fat made the wicker creak. With an elegant, persuasive hint of the silver-plated handle, he indicated to her the empty chair next to him.

Katharina smiled, looked away.

The slim waiter, with the threadbare jacket, came up to her. She looked carefully at him. Nothing impressed her, as if the man had no face.

"Excuse me, but . . . The professor is a regular. He

moves with difficulty. He's asking me if . . . Would you like to have tea with him?"

She was not surprised, the stammering of the waiter convinced her. Without answering she stood up and sat down next to the professor.

He smiled, but his lips were not visible. And she found herself listening with a childish curiosity.

"Thank you for coming," the man said. "My legs don't allow me to move with agility . . . I wanted to speak to you yesterday . . . but I was sure I would see you again." And, without waiting for an answer that did not come, he continued:

"You are familiar with loneliness . . . In this you are like me. There is the suspense of waiting about you, it is a weight that follows inertia . . . Your eyes float so pale, wherever emptiness takes them."

She had settled down in the wicker chair and calmly, as if she thought it unimportant, replied:

"I've come back here for a specific reason. A hearing is due in a few days . . . Even if this keeps me busy . . . there are too many signs that I cannot dismiss . . ."

They were looking at the silence that surrounded them.

"The plaster has been covered with too many coats of paint," she carried on, "perhaps they wanted to fix the tangle of shapes. They put waterproof paint on the façades of houses as well . . . as if they were boats."

"I remember your face," he interrupted her, "you were sitting at a corner table . . . you were pale."

"Are you here as an observer? Is that why you wear such thick glasses?" Katharina asked in one breath. "Am I really not allowed to know?"

"Why do you say this to me?" the man asked in return and shaped his non-existent lips into a smile.

"Yes," she slowly whispered, "someone has convinced

me that names don't matter . . . Maybe yours is an exception?"

"Names don't matter, and mine is no exception," he confirmed. He was strangely good-natured, a grandfather coming back to things patiently. She became suspicious. Kindness, especially if unexpected, always annoyed her.

"You must be right . . . I am so tired . . . and aware that I can't escape, even from you . . . I don't know if you really saw me, it may be . . . Have you heard about the crime? . . . the Serbian girl . . ."

"Yes, I've heard," the man said and moved a little, changing position. "May I ask you something?"

"She appeared to me suddenly, from behind the wall of shoulders that surrounded her. She was wearing a simple dress and her legs had been uncovered in the fall, white . . ."

"Did she die straight away?"

"I don't know, they carried her away."

Katharina pulled the zip of her handbag, opened it, closed it, opened it again. The man lowered his eyelids.

"I couldn't pull myself away . . . her body was stretched out . . ."

"The girl's story was part of you, wasn't it?"

"In those eyes not yet closed, lived something beyond fear . . . It must have been that detail . . . those eyes had become even brighter . . ."

"Well," he exclaimed, "in this very city . . . how can one think that silence can be broken . . . one walks the same streets . . . the mountains are the same, the sky . . . but there is a shadow which corrodes like saltpetre."

"Yes, I felt it in my stomach."

"Nevertheless you have been thinking of your project."

"Not really . . . I need to speak to the lawyer . . . but

so far he has been delayed . . . today we live with delays
. . . they change our lives uncaringly . . ."

"Have the proceedings already started?" the man
showed interest.

"Yes, the lawyer said: 'It will be over in a few days'
. . . But everything becomes clogged up, movements slow
down."

"As when we discover we are sick," he commented.
"An unexpected sign, almost imperceptible . . . and it
spreads . . ."

"It's something I find hard to understand . . . Perhaps
it's destiny, that is to say, reality."

"She was young, wasn't she?"

"She was twenty . . . and she didn't want to wait . . .
someone nearby was saying 'One can't live with this
obsession . . . working in the city and having to return
at night' . . ."

"I have observed your movements for a long time," he
interrupted, "your way of sitting down . . . your eyes . . .
Thoughts wear themselves out. Life must be captured in
your eyes, in their transparencies, in your hands."

"The Serbian girl," Katharina continued, "thought that
love would dismantle the wall . . . The daffodils that the
Slav girls offer amongst the mirrors are not damaged by
the air of the cafés . . . That look was hiding a story . . ."

"Had she made a choice?"

"I think you could say that. You must be able to look
into the depths of the damk spots, and then they shine
again."

"Just like the master glassworkers . . . they distil the
thickest of mixtures, and then they find in this the purest
of transparencies."

"That's true," Katharina admitted. "At the beginning
there is only sand which in the workshops does not reflect

the light of water and air. Fire alone cannot melt it and liberate its rays of light."

"You have to mix it with soda and marble to make it melt," the man specified. "Then arsenious dioxide and boric acid refine the molten combination."

"But from the flow of that liquid nothing transparent is revealed, no clear filament breaks off."

"The mixture shines," he continued, "when minium is added to it, with potassium carbonates and barium."

"All such dull substances," Katharina observed. "In the same way truth surfaces through the filigree of speech."

"And there are chips of oxidized metals," the man confirmed, "which add the distinction of colour to the transparency. Besides cadmium and carbon disulphides, add uranium and cerium oxides and you'll have yellow; more copper oxide with selenium and gold and the colours will turn bright red and ruby. Other oxides will make the intense colours liquid, the blue will shine with cobalt and copper oxide, the amethyst with manganese oxide, the green with chrome oxide."

"It's really like interrogating a memory," Katharina murmured.

"It's a balance," he added slowly, as if weighing small quantities of elements, "a subtly measured dosage. Nobody has discovered better than glass artists how to produce this marvel. Miniaturists and painters on wood might mix vegetable and mineral colours, measured like theorems and rhymes. But the glass game takes all the risk."

"I'm thinking of the opal . . ."

". . . that is both clear and cloudy . . . and thick like milk when the compounds of fluoride dissolve in it, acidulous like anise with arsenic and lead, alive with the light of pearls and silk if it absorbs sodium sulphate."

"These indecisions that dissolve shade and intensify light," Katharina concluded, and her look ran across shining showcases again, "are not only in the grain of matter, in how it mixes, turns into amalgam or preserves particles like volatile dust. They are also apparent in the skill of the layers. A patina of opaline and a transparency of colour. A double bottom, an eye that cuts through a veil. The masters of Nuremberg stir black patterns inside the brilliant solidity of crystal."

"You question things that others neglect . . . and you like stopping in cafés . . ."

"Yes, I like cafés, I can isolate myself."

"That's right, one catches the essential . . . Leaflets from the café tables . . . filled with short symbols like algebraic signs . . . remarks that get worn out . . . Don't you find that in every phrase there is already an act of plunder?" And he added slowly, looking at her: "You young people must know . . . everything comes alive and moves in conflict . . ."

"Before I had the baby . . . Friedrich . . . I prepared and pursued experiments in the laboratory," she explained, wanting to draw a clear line between herself and the man. "Physics does not come into it, maybe, it's just one of my obsessions . . ."

"On the contrary, I think that it is a good explanation, cities develop within economics, within calculations of the figures, just like reactions . . ."

"During these last few days, walking around the city," Katharina continued, "I have thought about the exterminations carried out . . . just on the outskirts of this city . . . the sea still seems to be veiled with ash . . . and nobody wants to talk about it . . ."

"This city is sinking into the shadows . . . with its factories and silent sirens. There are no descendants . . ."

"Perhaps they would not be able to stand the accepted silence," she concluded in a low voice, turning her eyes beyond the window, towards the white city.

The man was silent. Then, observing the effect of his words, asked:

"What can be saved and taken away?"

"Perhaps this very uneasiness."

"It's all much simpler when one recognizes the weaknesses . . . One cannot understand further . . ."

"Yes," the man admitted, "even numbers amplify words but they do not succeed in expressing a total harmony . . . It's the same with sounds . . .", he started, "one always ends up by coming across something that's lacking."

"Fear," she corrected. "It is this fear that has pushed many to a duel with the mirror."

"Fear," he repeated. "This reminds me of the mathematician who wrote his life's work on the night before his duel."

"He must have known suddenly what he wanted. He knew his dawn . . . I don't think there are explanations for this kind of discovery . . ."

"Our glance," the man resumed, his voice flowing on as if from a tape, "does not contemplate many variables in the experiments . . . We are like those animals deprived of eyes, such as the *Proteus anguinus*, which live in the Karst caves in the darkness of water and stone . . . Any clear outlines disintegrate . . . Of dreams, too, there remain only descriptions that are more and more fragile . . ."

What sadness I feel for the cranes lined up along the wharf," Katharina noted. "Have you seen? They are bent, leaning over their idle arms . . ."

"Why don't you give up? . . . You keep on thinking of infinity as a growth without end . . . And the truth is in mirrors that have been scratched . . . those useless cranes themselves . . ."

The man stopped talking, he was tying together the threads of a demonstration.

The air was saturated, stifling. She found herself in the atmosphere of an experiment. Something had not worked correctly in the physics laboratory. Years spent in the stale air and then nothing, bubbles of dispersed vapour.

It was a stifling day in August.

The knocking on the door was getting louder. Sharp blows on her temples covered in sweat. Fragmented drops of water were sliding down.

The window onto the garden was shut, the glass clouded.

The tropical plants had taken root, something was sprouting from the earth at the stone roots. Chemistry did not concern them. They were immobile like monuments, they were not afraid of the wind.

The darkness was thicker. The man looked for some tea in the now empty tea-pot.

"There is a cost in every transaction . . . Look, the season is full of vigour and it darkens already, even if the light is warm . . ."

"Yes," she nodded, "words condense like vapour in this café . . . they form so many layers . . ."

Beyond the glass door the city was even whiter, undecided between a dense light and a bright mist which gave the stone a green reflection.

She rubbed the corner of her eyelid, a numbness prevented her from focusing the contours of things.

"The growth of this port," she said quickly almost as if measuring a project, "must have fitted a series, concluded it . . ."

"There wasn't any terror yet in algebra . . ."

"For the city to move in this direction," she objected, "was the idea of Maria Theresia and Ioseph II."

"Maria Theresia did not come to the city, did not see the work . . . They say that she hated the sea . . ."

"And yet she contributed so much to things maritime."

"She must have foreseen a problem . . . How could an ongoing industrial development have kept an unchanging order?"

The blood was pressing against her temples. She reacted as when one is pushed forward by a blow.

"It happens like this," she said. "If the wind's strength is funnelled into a narrow street . . . Something suddenly expands, breaks the lines of the diagrams . . . The marble, too, inflates and deteriorates . . ."

"Some generations thought that harmony would prevail in the city . . ."

"In fact, they thought it was solid since they saw it grow laboriously from different roots and languages . . ."

"They were under an illusion . . . The gods had returned . . . above the houses the sky, the wind and the rain were capturing a warm life, like the ships in the port . . . The insurances should have taken fear out of it," the man said, his eyes hidden by the lenses. "But the experiment could not succeed . . . Against the killing of Franz Ferdinand there was no insurance . . . You know that, you have studied the figures in the crisis . . . An explosion leaves those who have reduced life to a pragmatic boredom incredulous . . . and it is order that is burned."

The early years in the physics laboratory. Those knocks on the door still resonated.

She had broken the drowsiness of the sultry air and opened the door. At that sleepy hour the institute was deserted. A little man wearing a grey apron, the new cleaning assistant, was holding her wrist tightly and, walking leaning forwards as if about to fall, he took her into Room 8.

She had not seen anything else. The Serbian doctor had hinted at some trauma. His arm was around her shoulders and the palm of his hand protected her eyelids. "Was it not in August, Katharina? It was hot and for the first time you were not able to see."

The chair had fallen over by the force of the push and the blow to her throat; thrown further away it hit the window, which was now swinging against the lit lamp. The vertically inscribed sheets were curling up in the heat; notes scattered by the caprice of chance. Over that random succession of letters and spaces an open pen had let its ink run out. The wastepaper basket was empty. The wind was beginning to move the stifled air and the vertical texts were scattered about. In the garden the letters would have burrowed into the hard ground like fertile seeds and would have exploded under the roots. Only fire would have scattered the sharp, white stones, splinters of bone forgotten even by the wind.

She hid the papers with the rush of a gull in winter. The telephones broke the humid silence of a distant August afternoon.

"Eels," the man said, freeing himself from the images which besieged them both, "will carry on darting down a stream, fast, as far as the promised point of the sea . . . this neverending instinct never stops."

"But for those who listen to this beating," she thought aloud, "departure is without return."

Outside the dust blew up against the windows. Passers-by were becoming distant and out of focus, like cloth dummies with stiff geometric movements.

A dark car pulled up quickly, just in the shade of the horse-chestnuts. A pale man with hands gloved in black leather was driving it. The engine stayed running; curiously, it did not make any noise.

The car glided slowly down the avenue, taking, with the subtlety of the wind, the man with the silver walking-stick. She just had time to see his furry wool-covered hand grip its handle.

She stiffened. The pain in her hands started again, she tried to rub them, the blood was stopping at her wrists. She squeezed hard on the marble of the table. Perhaps it was just a dream and she was running along streets whose walls were too high. But the waiter came and brought her the bill.

12

The narrow street with the sharp-cornered houses was in front of her, it oppressed her. She felt as if she were wearing tight shoes, or was it the effect of the converging houses, of the corners?

She recognized the corner where the road started to rise. In order to concentrate she stopped, stood up straight, her face raised. Two windows closed their shutters with a bang. A dark figure hung something bright on a washing-line, nappies. A girl with prominent cheek-bones pulled a long red string with a small celluloid boy doll at the end. She tried to pick it up, it had no eyes. But the girl pulled on the red string and the doll disappeared inside the house.

It was like being back in the physics laboratory. She was crossing the corridor and entering the darkroom. Her retina was being crushed from all directions and the pain caused her to see a yellow flicker, coloured stars by the thousands. She followed the man dressed in white into the storeroom with the glass cupboards. In a glass test tube was an already-formed tiny shape, she did not remember the eyes, maybe the eyes needed time. Or maybe the glass contained only a bent root.

The short distance between the laboratory and the

darkroom allowed the persistence of consonants of that incoherent code that is the alphabet of sight. Dark spots were dancing in front of her, breaking up and their fragments taking on strange images. She tried to join them into a whole, with the tenacity of a restorer of antique china. Even for the most skilful artisan it would have been difficult to put the dancing figures back in the right place. The rhythm of the gestures was compromised, it was enough to have one minute particle missing and an arm or an ankle would not express the sense that the dancer wanted.

She, too, had lived like those dancers on antique vases. On that distant night long ago, when Leopold had helped her escape, her husband's left forearm was forming some incoherent movements. Everything had started after the shouts that one could still hear beyond the closed windows and the bushes shaken by the wind. Sleep, before calming her down, would take the shape of a shadow, always the same one for years.

Before the shouts, she had perceived the unsteady steps, the insistent limping of his left foot. The spasmodic language and letters of the alphabet piled up on top of each other as in childish games. Then came the familiar step of Leopold: he was coming to lock up the room before the other could enter. And when the massive door would not yield, he would curse both her and the terrible illness that was melting his brain, like snow.

She turned immediately behind an old fabric shop. The street now ran straight past the big insurance buildings. "What a parodoxical invention," she thought. Behind those walls life managed to take on a calming appearance.

"What a gamble life insurance is . . . Our relatives are the Others and they smile happily at us because we insure our death for the benefit of their lives." It had always been like this, one insured empires. "But is nobody thinking of anything against the shadows of the night, when life becomes evanescent and elusive?" she asked loudly. "Yes, the eels, haven't I got an appointment with the boy and the lost puppy?"

"Tomorrow, at the mouth of the river," he had said. The boy would drop the nets and together they would wait for the eels. She had eaten them once, they were tasty but too greasy. She had had to drink slivovitz; it was in a yellow bottle similar to the one she had seen in the shop of the little Serbian woman. A slivovitz made by Slovenian farmers, it had all the smells of the woods and was easy to drink, like water, it did not burn, it gave a strange feeling of security.

She was walking and glancing upwards. She was looking for the clouds, but her glance met telephone lines twisted round some bare tree. The windows, like old flattened scars, made holes in the cement of the grey façades. The plaster had lost its original colour, a mixture of cancerous dust had disfigured the eaves worn away by the wind. The light fell straight onto those stage-set houses, without illuminating them.

Suddenly, as if she had just been walking in a desert, she found herself in a noisy open space, like a small country market on the day they sold plants. The colours of the flowers were so bright, the chrysanthemums yellow spots of solid colour.

"Water," she thought. "First, I must know where to find water."

The carpark attendants were very busy. "I have come on the wrong day." And she started to walk in, past the large entrance.

At the office where one goes to find out the exact location of the dead, it was not busy. It was the lunch hour, or else other people knew their way about.

She mentioned the name, she was afraid to ask at the office. She had never succeeded in completing her inquiry, something was always missing from her request. "No'l xe più là, bisogna zercar nei archivi veci. In 'sto momento no posso, se la vol spetar . . . No go tempo, la capissi . . . Me dispiasi, se la veniva mezo minuto prima . . . Xe serado. Me par che i misti xe al campo XIII. Cossa la ga dito? El iera nato a Vienna? La provi a vardar de quela parte, lo troverà subito. No xe fiori, la sa, non vien nissun, xe i misti . . ."[1]

". . . Invece da lori, dai ebrei, la vedi lassu', xe un muro che dividi, non la pol passar. Se devi andar fora, dopo ghe xe una riveta e là xe lori."[2]

She climbed alongside a wall, reached a bridge and

---

[1] "No, its not there any more, you must look in the old archives. At this very moment I can't, if you'd like to wait . . . I haven't time, do you understand . . . I'm sorry, if you had come a minute earlier . . . It's closed. But it seems that the mixed ones are in field No XIII. What did you say? Was he born in Vienna? Try looking over there, you will find him immediately. There aren't any flowers, you know, nobody comes, it's the mixed lot . . ."

[2] "On the other hand with them, with the Jews, you see up there, there is a wall that divides, you cannot go through. You need to go outside, further on there is a bank and that's where they are."

went into the avenue. She approached an old lady who kept murmuring: "Tutto te impesta, odor de pino fa mal de testa."[1] She spoke to her, and the woman answered without looking:

"No savaria ben se xe'l greco, forse 'l giudio, la provi."[2]

She noticed that a boy leaning on his scooter was watching her. He looked like the boy with the rust-coloured pullover. "They are all the same," she thought, "an army of boys made from one mould."

She straightened out her skirt and the boy was still observing her. She then asked:

"Is it here . . . are you sure?"

"Yes, but you have to ring the bell."

"I can't find it."

And the boy, without moving closer, motionless:

"It's on the right, behind the ivy, a bit higher up."

The gate opened. She had only lifted her hand ready to ring. That had been enough, perhaps someone behind the window was waiting.

The black wings folded themselves back against dark bushes. Each rustling was deadened by the tangled growth of plants. She was engulfed by the dampness of laurel hedges.

A girl as slim as a mulberry branch appeared and pointed to the avenue. She walked along it, listening to her steps on the sharp gravel. She tried to make her footsteps lighter to soften the crushing of the stones, without success.

---

[1] "It pollutes everything, the smell of pine gives you headaches."

[2] "I don't really know if this is the Greek part, maybe it's Jewish, try and see."

The girl had come down and asked in a gentle voice:
"Can I help you? Who are you looking for?"

The smell of the hedges, and of wax, stunned her. She
covered her eyes with her forearm waiting for the name
to come back clearly. The gentle voice had sucked it up
again like a sponge, without a noise.

"I can't really remember . . . I want to look at these
names. Is it possible?" And she leant her chin against her
neck with a sigh.

The brightly dressed girl walked away lowering her
eyes.

Suspended lives surrounded her. The steps were en-
cumbered by a tangle of plants. The hedges were high
but a blackbird passed to and fro picking in a rhythmic
way all around a section of the earth.

An intermingling of languages met on the stone.

A copper vase was overturned, originally it had been a
shell, she read the name of the soldier who had engraved it.

The blackbird was not afraid of her presence. He put
his beak into the rich earth, in search of food. His nest
was somewhere else, and he worked on industriously, his
search reducing memory to an unbearable burden.

She turned her back on the hard hieroglyphs, and the
blackbird stopped pecking the earth, and began to sing
obsessively. Its voice was behind the hedge and she
answered in a low voice:

"Du hast etwas unerledigt zurückgelassen.
Ich gehe fort und lese verstohlen die letzten Namen,
die von der Ferne kommen."[1]

---

[1] "You have left something in suspense./I go away secretly and read
the latest names/that have come from far away."

She went out furtively, hardly compressing the gravel. The door from which the slim girl had appeared was closed. She merely turned towards the fir-tree that covered the piece of ground she had come to find. The gate opened; she was again surprised by the lack of noise. Then the heavy iron wings closed again behind her.

She thought she might find the boy with the moped, but the street was empty. She changed direction, she did not want to go back across the large open space and the clutter of the flowers with their excessively bright colours.

She did not have a watch, but it was not long before her appointment with the boy.

The profiles of the mountains and the sea were long level lines in the sky.

She walked up paths as steep as ladders, houses became more and more infrequent.

The boy waited near the abandoned building site. They did not stop, but carried on towards that piece of land where every contrast of ground and nature was distinct and where it seemed improbable that one could trace a frontier line.

A few Slav peasant women were coming down. Amongst the stones their figures seemed to get bigger suddenly, to transform themselves in that feared wind that sweeps across the gorges and down to the sea.

The boy hurried his steps, he wanted to reach the border.

Katharina tried to see a logic in that uneven country. The layers were broken up, overturned, dark bands veined white rock-faces, the dusty ground had streaks of blood and water running down like tears. "A geology of catastrophes," she thought. She wanted her red scarf, it had been left tied to the café chair where the girl had been killed.

They started to run, the ground sliding under their feet. Katharina was the first to fall; she got up again. But the boy also ended up stumbling. They helped one another with their hands but they slid along with the ground.

They reached a higher point, formed by a white rock rising like a lance. They could not stop themselves sliding down. They looked at each other, desperate. They tried to walk around the obstacle; that was even harder, the ground became slimy like a marsh. They were falling and did not have anything to grip. With nothing to hold on to, they were going to hit their heads on the jutting-out rocks.

The boy had some advantage over her because his shoes were heavier, and he had been able to wedge them against a plank, not particularly strong but driven in amongst some stones.

They decided not to obstruct each other. She was trying to get away from the boy so as not to discourage him. She threw herself face down, sliding on her side. Fear paralysed her. From that position she could see; there was no possibility of getting out of there, if they carried on sliding they would surely fall into the void.

She did not want to tell the boy that it was impossible. She threw a glance at the reddish patch of the pullover and cried out:

"Stop. Let's rest for a while. There must be a path."

At that moment the boy, too, saw the closeness of the precipice:

"Stay where you are, don't move."

"Yes," she echoed, "don't worry. If I don't move, nothing can happen to me." And she thought: "I could try to bandage my eyes. That way I could roll over and my eyelids wouldn't get hurt when the barbed wire hits them." But she did not add anything. Something had to happen. Under her the smell of the ground was very strong. "If I get an allergy attack . . ." To get rid of the terror that this idea had caused, she tried to think of how they came to be there. "The ground ran smoothly just before, it must have been a large bit that had moved and created the trap. And the plank that was supporting the boy kept swaying. It's no use." She turned and looked with dilated eyes towards the empty sky, without a cloud.

In order to look upwards she had pressed her body hard against the ground, almost making a cavity. She tried to drive her hands and feet into the soft earth. Then she felt something hard under her back, she imagined it was a large, flat stone like a moon. Slowly, careful not to lose what little support she had, she succeeded in pressing her bottom against the rock. She had to dig in her feet so as to push with sufficient force. She managed it. It was now she who cried to the boy:

"Stay where you are. We'll make it."

She analysed the new situation quickly, looked at the boy, immobile, in the same place:

"Stay where you are. I'll make another hole. Near here it should slide less. I'll find another stone. Then we'll let ourselves down sideways. It's only a few metres." She had become aware that something in that earth was helping her.

13

Klaus welcomed her when she came back to the hotel. And, without her asking anything, he added:

"Two telephone calls and a telegram for you, madam." He was leaning too far over the desk as he spoke to her, like a puppet that a string pulls as it wants.

Katharina smelt his acid breath and sensed the stickiness of his skin. The reddish moustache with mixed, thin hair, tormented by a frequent tic, stood out over his lips and allowed a glimpse of his shadowy teeth.

When he had stopped looking at her, he turned around to reach for her key and the messages. The telegram and the torn 'phone message slips, of a bluish colour.

She squeezed the hard and yellow paper of the telegram in the warm palm of her clenched fist. Her name was spelt wrongly. "As always," she thought, "perhaps it's not for me."

Klaus had walked out from behind the desk and was standing in front of her. His colourless eyes fixed themselves on her shoes dirty with dried mud.

"Have you been out? To the other side?"

She did not answer. She followed his look beyond her shoes. Her stockings were laddered on her red ankles. She was surprised to find herself in such a state, a short while ago everything had seemed normal.

While turning her back to go to the lift she asked, trying to make her voice appear neutral:

"How is Leopold?"

The young porter, already looking after the new guest, did not hear her, and bent over the Japanese gentleman's small map:

"*Would you like anything else, sir?*" he asked ostentatiously in English, as if it were his exclusive property. And he smiled at a foreign lady who had come up to him.

"*I'm looking for a street not far from the sea. But perhaps it isn't on the map.*"

"*This district exists only in name. The new district is much more interesting.*"

"*They advised me to look for a villa.*"

"*Oh, I beg your pardon,*" he noticed her still waiting. "*Perhaps the lady was before me. I didn't notice, I'm sorry.*"

"*No, No. I've already finished.*"

For some days at different moments she had been wrapped in a cloud of sand and her eyes had suffered sudden redness. Then the heat of her head became unbearable.

The day she had arrived seemed long ago.

She looked again at the furniture lined up against the walls. She noticed the lack of objects. Any kind of ornament would have been a relief, but in hotel rooms there is nothing superfluous.

The bed looked at her untouched, the covers stretched as if with elastic. The white purity of ironed sheets repelled her; the mirror on the dressing-table made it look twice as wide.

The floor, rather unstable, produced a vibration in the mirror which amused itself by fragmenting her.

By the window, barely covered by curtains dark

with dust, a box made of imitation wood echoed her steps on the parquet floor with prolonged sounds. "How can something so banal," she asked herself, "be so irritating?"

There must have been a loose connection in the wire as the fridge went off and on continually. She firmly pulled out the plug. As a reaction, the door opened showing the inside, a safe space for the night-time traveller. The small bottles shook a bit, then quietened down, conscious of being unable to exist but for the insomnia of some of their guests.

She would have liked to bite into an apple, even a old one, like those that Bertrand Smoleck had left. "How difficult it is to want something in these places."

She turned her attention to the untouched suitcase. The dress brought for the hearing was tidily folded.

She took the red envelope containing the documents out of her overcoat pocket. The message on pale blue paper read: 'Tomorrow 9 a.m. first hearing Room 5. Juvenile court. Osermann, Lawyer.' With her hand she slowly flattened the paper and the dress, so that it would all be in order. The suitcase shut without a click.

Then she took the letter and, with the same hesitation as the one who had written her name, opened it:

Dear Katharina,
The night you arrived I could not say anything to you. But I know that you recognized me. Your pale pupils were lively like those of the boy when he asked me to bring him close to the sea, closer and closer. He kept asking if the sea was going to remain in the same spot even after he had grown up. He was afraid that the monsters would swallow it and reduce it to dry land.

Tomorrow morning when you get up you, too, will be able to see that the sea has not moved away. But it is not the same any more, its waves have become yellow and instead of shiny stones there is now rubbish.

Do you still keep the pink stone that you called 'luck'? When you had doubts you used to stroke it, and it became smoother and pinker.

I know that they have given you the suite no. 108, the one on the corner. It is the same one that the Count wanted last spring. Unlike you who were so moved that you did not say anything to me, he immediately said coldly: "How come you are still here, Leopold? At your age you ought to have a house," and patted me on the shoulder pretending a warm-heartedness he had never shown. I asked him about the child and he did not answer. I managed, however, to see something in his shiny bag and to know the reason for his visit. I cannot tell you much. Because of the rush I had left my glasses in my apron. But I saw the official documents and read the headings that said: "Juvenile court . . . examining magistrate . . .' So I can tell you something that may be of use to you.

You know, not very long ago in the old city I saw again the young men dressed as cooks selling radishes. But it's such a long time since I saw the Friulians with their breast-plates, you liked them because they had copper kettles hanging on their chests and you used to say that they did not sell pears but sounds.

In San Giacomo one can still hear the odd call: 'more col brodo, puina, puina fresca'.[1] You may not remember these things, and you'll think that I have grown older and more tired. But I want to cheer myself up. There is still the odd salesman of 'brustolini' and here, by the hotel, the woman who sells a bit of everything keeps passing

---

[1] Mulberries with syrup, fresh cream cheese. (Tr.)

backwards and forwards in front of the glass door. You cannot miss her because she wears a flared, coloured skirt, and among the many things for old customers she keeps the odd pumpkin seed, a sou's worth of 'fiepe'.

Tomorrow morning you have to go to the concierge at number 9. You must ask her from me to let you have the papers. You see, I have managed to remember the odd name and other details and I have copied them down, I knew that I would see you again. I've left them with siora Lena for safety. On the night I helped you escape, his cries had become impossible. There has always been a mystery over the keys of the yellow room, they had disappeared for years, and only that very night did somebody find them.

Fate has been good to me this time, too. I should have left as from tonight, they had wanted to send me away for a long time, they say that my legs are no longer nimble and I'm stumbling. I stayed on because Klaus had not come back, these youngsters are always on holiday. But I'm not well at all. Try to be strong and you'll be able to keep the child. Goodbye Katharina, tomorrow you will see the sea again with me, I'll squeeze your hand and we'll look again at our coloured stones.

your very own Leopold

The envelope also contained a sheet written in larger letters, as if the hand had wanted to correct it. The note concerned the papers of siora Lena.

I remember a letter written by Countess Irene. To conceal it she would change its hiding place. It was in the false bottom of the box used for keys that she gave me to look after, when she became ill. I did not want to read it, not for years. Then the Countess died. I already knew what was written. She had tried to prevent the marriage of her son, but his threats became stronger and stronger and she was becoming weaker and weaker . . . and then she was hoping, like all mothers. Maybe the old doctor is still alive, a word from him would prove that you could do nothing but go away. I knew the course of the illness, Countess Irene had warned me: "he will start to lock everything and to hide the keys . . . he will stay for longer periods in the room with the showcases . . . he will suspect everyone, he will have violent attacks alternating with moments of absence . . . the words will be broken, incomplete." And she warned me more than once: "my old Leopold, you have to be careful . . . and you will also help Katharina." Your pregnancy was not foreseen and I myself, God forgive me, on the night the horse died, was hoping you would lose it. But Friedrich is not afraid of anything, he is a nice healthy boy.

She was still wearing the overcoat as she went into the big bathroom. She ran the water. She did not want to get wet, she just wanted noise and steam to fill the room.

She sat on the edge of the bath. The imitation mosaic was beginning to steam up, slowly in contrast to the mirror over the washbasin. She had a strange impulse, stood up and wrote: 'Will they give me the child tomorrow?' But she hated questions without answers and wiped it out.

She heard the siren of a ship. Yet, ships were rare, maybe it was just an alarm set off without reason.

Carefully she closed the inside shutters of the long windows. This way the bathroom kept the noise all to itself.

Small, dry drops were hanging from the ceiling. They were either paint or perhaps the water in the apartment above had leaked during her absence. The ceiling was high but one could see. The drops already hanging would not have touched her head.

At her feet was her small, round leather bag. It must have been searched by many hands, she was sure of that. Even Bertrand Smoleck had given in to the common curiosity to look inside: she had seen him during the night.

She lit a cigarette and threw the packet at the bin, but her hand trembled and made it fall into the toilet bowl, still of old porcelain. She made a gesture of irritation: "Das macht man nicht, Katharina, das ist deiner nicht würdig."[1]

She got up and flushed the water. For a moment the red packet turned in the noisy spiral of water, and then disappeared.

Someone was knocking at the door. A small maid smiled at her:

"Oh madam, I was going to tell the management as I had not seen you go out. I've been knocking for a long time. Are you not feeling well, perhaps?"

"No . . . it's because of the water. When it's running, you know how it is . . . and outside there is a lot of noise . . ." She blushed and turned her face towards the window.

The woman came close to the bed, which was bandaged up like a mummy. Her small hands opened the covers with agility and everything was suddenly ready.

During the night her damp hair curled up like the waves that trouble the sea in the morning. She couldn't reach the line of rocks. Her arms were making an effort but

---

[1] "One doesn't do that, Katharina, it's not worthy of you."

the water did not give way and the movement had a contrary effect. The water obstructed her arms and her eyes saw an imposing head with a curly wig. A massive nose, bent over the mouth, divided the reef. Nothing supported the two rocks and yet something joined them. On the sand a body, white and bloated.

The water was pressing against her eyes, and enlarged objects. The splashes of waves, like inverted binoculars, brought details of the rock closer.

Now and then her arms gained strength and managed to free themselves from the chain formed by the water.

At one point she became aware that behind her a large dolphin was swimming fast. She was not afraid, even when it came closer. With blows of its tail it pushed her towards the rock, then it turned over and its nose appeared where its tail had been. It gave the impression of having two heads, but it was simply because it was moving from side to side, changing the position of its head with rapid movements. Suddenly she saw it no longer.

The sea had turned into a slimy marsh. She managed to drive her fingernails into a protruding rock that welcomed her, but, as soon as she had entered the cave, sharp points appeared and hurt her, only her face remained untouched.

The cavity widened in an unexpected way, out of all proportion. It was crumbled stone but it took the shape of a small monster made of fetid, reddish-coloured rubber. The enormous head was wrapped in a light mist, a shroud that gigantic and livid hands held against the chin.

Her arms were now resting, and the sweat disappeared. She tried to get out of the cave. Tiny men encircled her, spraying her with that reddish light that increased her sight. She could see her eyes in the projection opposite, and they reflected back like a razor. She fell again into the slippery mud.

At the edge of the marsh, in the little pool of water that was still left, the dolphin reappeared. By turning round, it made lazy waves in the pool that became larger and burnt like blazing petrol.

She slipped into the blue circle and the dolphin threw her back towards the bog. On the divided rock she found a stack of wood and lay down on it; it was as soft as feathers.

Meanwhile the dolphin was swimming away, its endless tail rose up like an unattainable tongue of fire.

The marshes had been allowed to dry up and had turned into land not yet planted, as if only recently ploughed. The friendly dolphin, before leaving, had hit the divided rock with its tail. The last thing to disappear was the enormous head with curly hair, a powerful nose and empty eyes.

She took a long time getting dressed. The room was quiet. From the wall nearby she could not hear the noise of the previous evening.

She was attentive to the slightest ticking. For her the wall was the border. She found herself having to confront the things that divided her and, to do this, she limited herself to paying attention to the noise of the people near her. Perhaps it wasn't much, but she would start by listening.

"In hotels," she thought, "one can be strangely close . . . be similar to those who breathe next to you." She had on occasion extended her stays because she had not perfected her fantasies and had not managed to guess the gestures of certain people. The curiosity, then, had sharpened and she had the feeling that there was nothing to divide her but a screen. She and 'the other' could observe each other any time, day and night. Sleep was becoming lighter, confused. Slumber suffered a slowness as grey as the nose of a mouse. She experienced a physical difficulty in recomposing the fragments between dream and reality. The only solution was to make a decision.

The same happened that morning as well.

It was early. The empty lift was exasperatingly slow. "They would do well to replace them, they'll do for a museum."

She ran along the soft, violet, worn-out corridors.

She went down the stairs with the flowery railings.

The young porter was not behind the desk. The hanging keys did not shine, nobody had polished them for a long time, only the clear morning brightened them up.

She caught a glimpse of the waiter at the far end of the hall, he was coming in with the breakfast trays. She saw his outline rather than his face, as he slid away behind the glass door.

She did not hand over her key with the impressive tassel. Nobody saw her. The hotel was asleep.

The wind covered her face with her light hair. "It's so fine that I have never been able to do anything but gather it . . . it's like Friedrich's . . . blond and flowing, it covered his forehead while he was asleep in the little bed with the lightly lacquered sides."

She was walking fast. Having left the sea behind her,

she could feel its breeze. The noise from the town increased, which pleased her.

She thought of Bertrand Smoleck. For a short while she had felt a vague longing, almost a discomfort, for not having listened to him. "Men," her grandmother would say," must always be listened to when they speak, if they say silly things it's better to let them get on with it." "But Bertrand Smoleck did not say silly things, only he could hear nothing but his own words . . . What can one do, grandmother, when a man does not hear your voice? For sure, he is a musician born in Berlin, and perhaps it's me making a mistake, they really must be a special race. Of course . . . feelings have nothing to do with music," she concluded, "he was right about that."

She had arrived at the crossroads, still in the old part, once more in front of the café of the crime. This was the street. "It's a persecution," she told herself, and clutched Leopold's letter in her fist. "It's not true," she tried to convince herself, "it must be an illusion. It's not possible that it is like this, this only happens in films."

She went into the café of the crime. With relief she noticed the absence of the lady in charge. At the cash desk was the man who had washed the blood of the Serbian girl from the pavement. She looked at him with firm eyes as if to make sure of that presence and as if, instead of asking for wine, she was looking for something owed to her.

The man recognized her, smiled at her, pleased to be seen at the counter, without his apron. He shut the till firmly and poured her some wine, looking pleased:

"This one is better," he said, "we just changed it today . . . You see, it's from a different producer . . . from upper Friuli."

149

Katharina drank almost in one gulp, she felt the pleasing bitter taste go down her throat, the smell of the crushed autumn leaves in her nostrils:

"Oh yes, it's really good. Perhaps a little too cold."

"You are right," the man admitted, "you are a real expert. But the fridge is always on maximum, I never know why."

"I would like to eat something, even just an egg. But I'm in a hurry. Tell me, I'm looking for number 9. Do you know the concierge?"

"I'm not sure," answered the man. "I think number 9 is the one with the lobby . . . or maybe it's a bit further . . . You'll spot it because of a smell of tanned leather and other things coming out of there."

"This is a young wine, isn't it? I like it."

"Come back, come back again."

Katharina smiled. "Again," she thought, "is a beautiful word." And she went out, with the address still in her clenched fist. "It's not right," she thought, "it doesn't matter, I will find it all the same."

She was in front of the staircase, as if she had flown. She noticed a smell of grease coming from the basement, grease and onions. "Goulash," and she pulled in the belt of the damp overcoat. She wanted to look at herself in her mirror, but she felt it too public. "And in any case I lost the mirror the day my leather bag was knocked over." She then rearranged her hair on the back of her head. "Pity, in the rush I forgot my glasses . . . I would have felt more at ease."

She pushed open the low door or it was the shutter that opened, she did not really understand. She was in a room in the dark, only a grey strip entered diagonally from the window and slid along the cement floor. One could hardly see anything. The room did not appear to have furniture, apart from a tall and narrow display cabinet near the door. The glass was misty, one could see cups mixed with pictures and books. All of this surprised her and she talked absent-mindedly, as when the attention is on something else. She was looking at a leather-bound book.

Behind the curtain there was someone, waiting, or maybe sleeping. 'I'm going away," she hesitated, "I'll come back tomorrow." Just then, from under a chair a dog yelped; it was shivering, it shivered a lot.

"It's not pregnant," the man behind the curtain said, "it has a tumor on its stomach, it's going to die. We need morphine, somebody to inject it . . . it will have to be killed . . . My wife has left, I'm ill, I can't do it . . . And you, what do you want in a place like this?" he shouted.

"Me? . . . I'm sorry, perhaps I made a mistake . . . I have come at the suggestion of Mr Leopold," she hesitated when pronouncing the name, she was afraid of spoiling it and of losing it forever. She repeated: "At the suggestion of Mr . . ." This time she used the surname. "Well, in this letter he told me that Mrs Lena, your wife I believe, keeps, he himself gave it to her, an envelope for me." She finished quickly.

Now she could see the man. The light from the opening had shifted to his body. He was wearing a T-shirt with a large collar like sailors wear. She could smell the sweat sticking to the skin on his stomach and to the patches of his hair that bristled like pins. He did not seem unwell, or rather she did not wish him to be. Only a smell hung around her forehead, filled her throat . . . the smell of alcohol.

The man was laughing. He had decided to make fun of her, she felt sure he was mocking her, and could not understand why.

"There is no envelope here," he shouted at her, "and my wife has left."

Outside the air was still. The courtyards. The stones on the streets shiny, pearls of frozen tears. The dust flown away, like dreams. Dust not so much hidden as lost in the wind.

At the crossroads the streets did not come together; rather, new directions opened up. She wanted to follow them, something would have become clear.

She took the short-cut she knew. Maybe it was not the shortest way, but those façades squeezing together, the low arc of the portico attracted her attention.

She brushed against the side of the piazza where the breath of the sea faded, and found herself at the beginning of Via Cavana.

From above a door a stone head was gazing at her. There was always somebody looking at her in the open. "I must not look up," she told herself. Further on a bare tree made a supernatural silhouette on a wall. That shadow was gesticulating from a high bench in a courtroom, and an arm stretched out towards her.

"Yes, I have something else to say," she reacted. The voice retorted: "You have not seen your son for a long time. You could have done so.

From the top of the houses windows were leaning out supported by frames of old wood. The glass was dumb like flakes of mica.

"They didn't let me . . . and I haven't enough documentation . . . but I'll get it . . ."

Some men came out of a door, stumbling about. They were talking loudly, laughing.

" . . . and then it's my body that wants it!"

No voices. Beyond the avenue the sea was a still line, of dark blue.

A waiter put a vase of large, yellow chrysanthemums on the side table in the hall.

She glanced again at the central desk in the hall and at the tufts of red tassles like dressed-up plumes that held the keys. Many of the guests must have gone out. From the distance that she was, the rectangular box seemed full. Each one of the room numbers showed its plume, in correct sequence.

She turned towards the mirror. Every tiny triangle composed and multiplied in front of her eyes all the plumes on the keys until they became long banners. "These oriental mirrors sparkle like mosaic floors in the basilicas when a veil of dampness covers them."

In the semi-darkness a bust kept its place. The dust had given it a fragile appearance. It had turned yellow like ivory, or maybe the sculptor had simply used faulty marble.

The American woman stopped coughing, with a glass of crushed ice in her hand she approached the bust and poked it with her forefinger. A circle of dust disappeared.

A Japanese man went by. "It must be my room neighbour." He smiled with his eyes, and they became a horizontal line, parallel to the wrinkles that divided his forehead, as he beat with the knuckles of his fingers against an empty bronze suit of armour. Satisfied, he picked up his plume and key. He did everything with quick movements and without stopping; even the lift was too slow for him.

Klaus was negotiating in a mixture of dialects with the person who was probably going to replace him; he would be having two more days off.

Behind the desk the telephonist's office had remained opened. The telephones were ringing; small red and blue lights came on. Her absence was prolonged, the shrill ringing built up as persistent as coughing.

Sitting sideways, she looked at the mirror.

The broken light enlarged the red and black gowns grouped together in an old painting with a black frame, small figures repeated in order to compose the geometry of a hearing, even if a touch of green at the back sought to alleviate the feeling of discomfort.

Three Americans were laughing loudly. The woman coughed, she was smoking with determination, the cigarette hanging from her cracked lips. The other two carried on laughing, as if the cough were a variety of laughter. They had turned their backs on the big window towards the sea and were looking only at the man behind the bar. He did not seem to mind but came with glasses filled with ice, put them down absent-mindedly and went back to the corner where the music was coming from.

Two tables away from the Americans a man was sitting, almost hidden by a palm. He had thinning hair with a bald, unpolished pate, like the clerics of the Middle Ages. He kept his eyes fixed on a point beyond the hall, but, above all, he was concerned about the small suitcase so close to his ankles that it seemed to be tied to them. Something was making him sleepy in spite of the laughter of the Americans, and no headline in the newspaper seemed able to awaken him. Only the *Zeitungsspanner* falling from his hands, stirred him: he would snap it back as if he were pulling on a fishing line. And this sequence, despite his trying to maintain discretion, revealed his face.

The man came nearer without her noticing it. He looked like the first lawyer. Besides, he had said it already: "I have nothing in particular, only a briefcase full of documents."

"Mr Osermann? I was almost thinking I would not see you again."

"Forgive me; it is, indeed, a delicate case." And he put the file on the little table pushing the vase aside. He pulled his folding glasses out of a small case.

Katharina understood; the explanation he was about to give would be involved and evasive and she would end up being hurt. "And then," she thought, "this way of arranging the papers, as if for a demonstration, reveals how far away we are from a solution."

"Mrs Pollaczek", he began, raising his voice, "do you have a specific reason for thinking it impossible to consider the matter of custody in a calmer way?"

"Me? Why do you ask me this? I would just like you to finish the case left open by the first lawyer." There was urgency in her words. "I beg you, there is nothing to consider, I cannot see why the hearing should be postponed . . . And then it would not give a good impression to the judge."

"Very well. However, you have been here a few days, you might have thought, you might have met with . . ."

"Yes," she interrupted him, she felt that he wanted to confuse her, "let's come to the decision."

"But why," he insisted, "this hostility to allowing certain things to resolve themselves in the fullness of time . . . And then it would be necessary to produce yet another document."

"I do not wish to think about it," she answered, allowing her tiredness to show. "Don't you think that it's already been a long time?"

"In any case, for the moment," the lawyer concluded, "the only thing we can do is to adhere to what the judge wants, and can provide."

"Oh, that is exactly what I wanted to know and what I feared," she said sharply, but the words sounded disconnected.

Mr Osermann drew his chair nearer, tapped the sheets to make the stack neat, and began to read those small letters, all alike and without any deletions. He emphasized some points as if they were loaded with questions but immediately carried on without waiting for objections.

In no way would that text that continued so monotonously be modified by anybody.

Katharina Pollaczek's eyes turned to the large windows. At that time of day they reflected the fine dust of the first mist.

14

The blue room. The doors and the windows of deep green. The wind outside strong and hot, very hot.

"If the wind stops . . ." the Algerian architect said to her.

"No," Katharina replied, "the wind won't stop."

They were waiting together in the night. They wanted to sleep. Then the car drove fast along roads full of olive trees. No light came to meet them, the European roads were far away.

They squeezed together under a white awning, immense, as if for an ancient performance.

"It's always cold at night," the architect said.

"Yes," she murmured like an echo, "the African nights . . ."

The white dome swayed every time a plane took off.

"Ours is delayed," he continued after a silence. "Dawn is coming slowly."

"Dawn is always different . . . like oblivion."

She turned her back, the light was hurting her pupils.

They walked up to the plane. The smell of a clump of trees nearby was penetrating.

Miles of desert under the shadow of the wings, the stirring of the sand. Only the suitcases were untouched, the European clothes were all that remained.

She looked with nonchalance at the big bag in the corner, deep in the dust. A past was buried there with, at the bottom, the change of shirt that she hadn't been able to find.

"It's a world without a face," Katharina said, wanting to interrupt the monotonous noise of the car along the track.

"This expanse is like the wall that we push against at birth and look for when we die. A resistance that allows us to feel pain."

The guide, swathed in dark cloth, seemed not to notice the bumps. His head was unmoving. He would only check now and then that the goat skin containing the water was still intact.

"One might not want to cross the desert by the only road."

"It's a road where the perspectives cross each other, like beams in a prism," the architect replied.

"And what about taking a short cut which veers off?"

"These traces are invisible, endless . . . But one can't escape them."

They stopped near some dark stones piled up without any order, an island in the middle of the sand.

"Look," he indicated, "on some of those stones are engraved the very first inscriptions."

"Indefinite like those traces."

"Yes, it is only in the absence of any point of reference that signs can be born."

The stones turned purple in the evening. The profiles of the mountains enclosed the scene where, with the quickening of the shadows, their legends could be performed.

Along the edges some shrubs with white and naked stems tempted her with their green leaves. She went to touch them. The guide shouted something to stop her and the architect translated the warning:

"They are poisonous plants; if they touch your eyes you go blind. Even the animals keep away from them."

"And yet it's the same wood which is used for huts, for fences."

"Yes, it doesn't burn, it stays white, unchangeable."

She saw again the same white in the eyes of the old man who could no longer drive the caravan; a clot beneath the scratched eyelids. The rustling in the sand at night was stronger, it touched the body in the same way as did the looks of the veiled, stationary figures. Those garments were like sand, one had to interrogate the whole series, they held the secret.

At the very end of the track the houses of red earth appeared.

The surface of the unbroken walls was scratched by vertical writing. She thought of the dark stones. Or perhaps the engraved lines simply reduced the glare of the sun.

Her voice repeated words that shortly before he had uttered to her in an Arabic as subtle as the wind. His long thin hands, and the knuckles of his fingers showed his Berber origin.

"No, you're wrong, it's my voice, my use of the Arabic language. My hands are like yours, admit it."

"Why do you wish that?"

"I don't wish it, I think it."

"But your skin, I can smell it, it has the same scent as the desert."

"You mean the smell of the sand," and he smiled.

Behind the emerald green door, the dust was increasing, or maybe it was the shadow of that plant outside whose name she did not know.

His eyes were scrutinizing her warm bosom, his voice a real Berber sing-song of a boy far away. She answered in her language, to him imcomprehensible.

The soft passive figure for a moment took on familiar features. She understood how much he had absorbed, without any limit of time. And perhaps he did not exist, perhaps he had never managed to exist near her.

She had fed him. Now a green force removed the well ordered stones. The body with the silky skin became detached and she thought again of the corroded features, that fragment that lived in spite of the distance with the silent pain of a thorn. Now she knew how to be free, to listen to music, to savour the perfumes, to walk. The sea had been crossed, she felt a body close by.

In the wind the ghosts accepted the invitation and approached the straw hut adorned with blue and green. They replied between the notes of the guitars and disappeared along the expanses of sand. Far away the cities with their houses, boulevards, churches must be asleep and even in those grey atmospheres the odd thread of sand would appear in the cracks. Frosty eyes had for a long time imposed silence and now in no way could inertia be overcome . . . the unravelling of the fabric was unstoppable . . . Obedience, respect, dance steps. Procedures, hearings. Sad glances sliding beyond fixed points.

The hot sand took away the last stifled cells to germinate further shadows. And the wind pursued it, relentlessly.